RACE
FOR THE
ESCAPE

ALSO BY CHRISTOPHER EDGE

The Many Worlds of Albie Bright
The Jamie Drake Equation
The Infinite Lives of Maisie Day
The Longest Night of Charlie Noon

RACE FOR THE ESCAPE

CHRISTOPHER EDGE

DELACORTE PRESS

Text copyright © 2022 by Christopher Edge
Jacket art copyright © 2022 by David Dean

All rights reserved. Published in the United States by Delacorte Press, an imprint of Random House Children's Books, a division of Penguin Random House LLC, New York. Originally published in the United Kingdom by Nosy Crow, London, in 2022.

Delacorte Press is a registered trademark and the colophon is a trademark of Penguin Random House LLC.

Visit us on the Web! rhcbooks.com

Educators and librarians, for a variety of teaching tools, visit us at RHTeachersLibrarians.com

Library of Congress Cataloging-in-Publication Data is available upon request.
ISBN 978-0-593-48601-6 (hardcover) — ISBN 978-0-593-48603-0 (ebook)

The text of this book is set in 12.25 pt Adobe Jenson Pro
Interior design by Andrea Lau

Printed in the United States of America
10 9 8 7 6 5 4 3 2 1
First Edition

For Alex

The true object of all human life is play.
—G. K. Chesterton

1

This is The Escape.

It looks just how I imagined it would look: a neon blade of a building rising above the dark windowless warehouses that surround it. LED lights shimmer across its mirrored surfaces as I approach, catching my reflection in a kaleidoscope of color.

I'm buzzing with excitement. This is my reward for working so hard: an evening of adventure at The Escape.

That's if I can find my way in.

I'm not sure at first if this is part of the game. I skirt the edges of the building, searching for the entrance, but all I can see is an endless wall of glass. It's as though whoever designed this building forgot to put in a front door, which is a bit of a problem if you want to pay them a visit. Maybe that's why they called it The Escape—because it's so hard to find the way out.

Then I spot it. Halfway along the wall, what I thought was a reflection is actually a revolving door, the sleek panels that are wrapped around the rest of the building bulging gently outward in a smooth curve of glass. I come to a halt in front of this door, my mirror image reflected in stereo. Stepping forward, I push against the right-hand panel, eager to get the game started at last.

It doesn't move. The door's locked.

Looking up, I see the black ball of a camera lens staring down from the ceiling, a red dot at its center. Someone's watching me.

I give a friendly wave to the camera.

"It's me—Ami Oswald," I say with a hopeful smile. "I'm here to play."

There's a moment of silence as I wait for an answer. Then the revolving door clicks as the lock is released. This first test passed, I push against the panel again, and as the door swings, I step inside The Escape.

The air feels instantly cooler, the low humming sound of the traffic outside replaced by a hushed silence as the revolving door closes behind me. I'm in some kind of lobby, a large circular space that looks like the bridge of a spaceship. The curved walls ripple with the same soothing patterns of color that shimmered across the outside, while the lobby is lit by concentric circles of lights that shine down from the ceiling. There's a round reception desk in the middle of this space, its surface gleaming with the same bright whiteness that covers the floor. It looks like you could fit a thousand people in here, but as I look around, there's only me.

I step toward the reception desk, hearing the sharp rap of my footsteps echoing back across the empty lobby. I thought there'd be somebody here to greet me, but as I reach the desk, the only thing I can see is a name badge left waiting for me.

AMI

Picking it up, I pin the badge to my top. At least they've spelled my name right—Ami with an "i," not a "y."

When he made the booking, Dad said that this place was home to the ultimate escape room. People call them escape games or locked-room adventures, but the way they work is always the same: a team of players is locked in a room together to solve the clues and puzzles they find before time runs out. I like solving puzzles, so Dad figured a trip here would be the perfect gift for me. But it looks like I'll be playing alone.

"Hello."

The greeting makes me jump halfway out of my skin.

I turn to see a girl standing right beside me. Her eyes are hidden behind shocking-pink sunglasses, but the smile on her face beams brightly. Dark braids fall loosely around her shoulders, and a handful of freckles dot her dark brown skin. She's wearing a cap-sleeved T-shirt with a vintage gaming console on the front, black-and-white checked pants, and neon-green sneakers. This girl looks seriously cool.

"Do you work here?" I ask.

Removing her sunglasses, the girl shakes her head and points to the name badge on her T-shirt.

"I'm Adjoa," she says. "I'm here to play the game—just like you."

I smile back at Adjoa; her enthusiasm is infectious. I feel the same surge of excitement that I felt when I first laid eyes on The Escape. Maybe this is going to be fun after all.

"So where are the others?" Adjoa asks, raising a quizzical eyebrow. "I thought we were supposed to be a team."

As if in reply, we hear the whirr of the revolving door and turn to see two boys entering the lobby. They look about the same age as me—the same age as Adjoa too, now that she's taken off her sunglasses and I can see how old she is—but apart from that I can't help noticing how different they seem.

The first boy moves quickly, his short blond hair turning ash-white beneath the lights as he strides purposefully toward us. His restless eyes dart from side to side.

"So this is the place?" he asks, his voice echoing across the cavernous space. "Doesn't look like much to me."

With his black hoodie and joggers, he looks like he's heading for the gym, although this is probably a wise choice of outfit. Escape rooms can make you sweat a bit, with physical as well as mental challenges to beat. You might find yourself dodging tripwire traps or crawling through a laser maze. It all depends on the theme of the game you play.

Across the lobby, the second boy is still standing just

inside the door, looking around in wide-eyed wonder. With his baggy gray sweater and khaki cords, he doesn't look ready for any kind of physical challenge. Not unless we're going to be escaping from the fashion police. But my eyes are drawn to the Rubik's cube that he's holding, his long fingers absentmindedly twisting its squares. Intrigued, I watch as the colorful patterns flickering across the faces of the cube mirror those still shimmering across the walls.

The first boy swaggers to a halt at the desk.

"Hi," I say, but the boy just ignores me, reaching across the desk to pick up two more badges that I didn't notice before. Pinning the one that says OSCAR to his hoodie, he looks over his shoulder.

"Hey!" he calls to the boy still dawdling at the door. "Are you Ibrahim?"

At Oscar's shout, the second boy nods. His dark scraggly hair is swept back from his face and his angular features shift into a pensive frown. "That's me."

Ibrahim hurries to join us, the cube still click-clacking in his hands. Oscar holds out the badge with IBRAHIM printed across the front.

"Thanks," Ibrahim says as he sets his Rubik's cube on the reception desk, the puzzle now solved, with each face showing a single color. Taking his name badge, he smiles shyly at the rest of us. "Are you all here for the game too?"

"Welcome to the team!" Adjoa says brightly, turning the full beam of her smile in Ibrahim's direction. "Do you think we should call ourselves the Awesome Foursome, or maybe the Fantastic Four? We need to pick a name that'll look good on top of the leaderboard."

"We don't need a stupid team name to win this game," Oscar sneers, but then a new voice chimes in with a suggestion.

"How about the Five Mind?"

Turning around in surprise, I see a girl standing on the other side of the reception desk. She doesn't look much older than me—twelve or thirteen maybe. Her straight black hair is cut in a sharp bob, dark eyes shining from beneath her bangs. It takes me a moment to work out what her name is, as her badge is lost among all the others covering her denim jacket. Then I spot it, nestled next to the smiley faces, superhero symbols, and CND signs.

MIN

"I mean, if this game really is as tough as people say it is," the girl continues, "we're going to have to put our heads together to win."

There's a silent pause as we all try to work out where she's come from. Shifting patterns of color flicker across the curved walls. The only door into this place is the one we all walked through, and I didn't see Min come in.

"I like it," Adjoa says, breaking the silence. "It's a pun, isn't it? Like a hive mind, where people share their intelligence?

There are five of us, and if we all work together then we'll be five times as smart."

Min nods her head. "Maybe even smarter," she says. "What do you think, Ami?"

I glance around the lobby, wanting to make sure nobody else is hiding. There are no more name badges waiting to be collected. Standing beneath the bright lights, Adjoa, Oscar, Ibrahim, and Min stare back at me. It looks like this is my team.

"Sounds good to me," I agree. "But when's the game going to start?"

And then the lights go out and the shimmering colors circling the walls dissolve in a burst of static. For a second I feel a flicker of fear, but it's swept away by an onrushing excitement as the face of a man appears.

It's starting.

Game on.

2

"Welcome to The Escape," the man says, his voice filling the space. "I am the Host, and you have been chosen to save the world."

He looks like the kind of man you always see reading the news on TV, his hair neatly trimmed and his features in perfect proportion. The walls of the lobby have been transformed into a wraparound media screen, and the Host is staring out from every surface. His short dark hair is flecked with gray, and the lines on his face crease to form a concerned expression.

"You are humanity's last hope," he continues. "I can only pray that you will succeed where we have failed."

He's making it sound like the end of the world, but I can't stop myself from smiling. This is how these escape games always begin—the game master setting up the story and explaining what you need to do to win. It might be breaking into a bank vault to steal a priceless treasure or searching a scientific laboratory to discover a secret formula. Every escape room has its own unique mission. And now he's going to tell us what *we* need to do to save the world. . . .

I glance around at the others, their faces lit by the light from the screen. Ibrahim peers intently at the Host, his head tilted slightly, while next to him Oscar stands with his arms folded across his chest. Catching my gaze, Adjoa flashes me an excited smile and then nods in Min's direction. I look across the group to see that Min's pulled out a notebook from somewhere and is scribbling furiously as the Host continues to speak.

"We need you to find the Answer."

I can hear the capital letter in his voice as a news ticker starts to scroll across the bottom of the screen.

Find the Answer. Save the world. Find the Answer. Save the world. Find the Answer. Save the world. Find the Answer.

"All you need to succeed is hidden inside The Escape. The puzzles you find and the challenges you face might seem impossible at first, but for you nothing is impossible. Look around carefully. Everything is part of the game. Use your mind to find the Answer. It's what we need to save the world."

Min looks up from her notebook. "If you want us to find the Answer," she says, "don't you need to tell us what the question is?"

I thought this was a pre-recorded video, but the Host pauses, his gaze turning in Min's direction.

"We have so many questions," he replies, shaking his head sadly. "And there are more asked of us each day. Burning questions, billion-dollar questions, but it's all now just a question of time. The clock is ticking—the countdown has begun."

Staring out from the screen, the Host's flint-gray eyes seem to fix on mine.

"Find the Answer," he says. "Find the Answer before it's too late."

I don't know what he means. He's talking in riddles, but I'm supposed to be good at solving those. Before I can get my brain into gear, I hear Oscar pipe up.

"Find the Answer, save the world, bada bing, bada boom." He snaps his fingers with a click that echoes around the room. "So what are we waiting for?"

There's a grinding metallic sound, and the face of the Host starts to split into two. I hear Adjoa gasp in surprise as the screens that circle the walls slide apart to reveal an open door. This must be the way into the first of the escape rooms—the place where this game really begins.

Beyond the door, the room is in total darkness, but Oscar is already striding into it. The curved walls of the lobby now shimmer with color again, scrolling arrows showing which way to go.

"I will be monitoring your every move," the Host says, his disembodied voice floating free as Ibrahim, Adjoa, and Min quickly follow in Oscar's footsteps. "The path you take through The Escape will lead you closer to me. Take nothing for granted. Question everything. The Answer might be found in the most unexpected of places."

I hurry to catch up with the others, heading for the darkness of the room.

It's time to save the world.

3

I take a deep breath, straining my eyes against the absolute blackness that surrounds me. I can hear noises in the darkness: the creak of floorboards and then a heavy thud that sounds like a door slamming shut.

I've never been afraid of the dark, but it's still kind of a relief when a light finally flickers to life, filling the space with a warm yellow glow.

We're standing in what looks like an attic. A bare bulb hangs from the ceiling, illuminating a sloping roof and white-plaster walls crisscrossed with cobwebs. And between these walls, piles of electronic equipment are stacked everywhere I look: ancient computer systems, keyboards, monitors, and hard-drive towers. A trail of rainbow ribbon cables snakes from the innards of a black trash bag, while another garbage bag looks like it's filled with CDs and DVDs, the silver discs spilling across the floor. There are cardboard boxes and old packing cases everywhere, all filled with even more tech.

Everything is covered in a thick layer of dust. This looks like the place old computers come to die.

Adjoa and Oscar are already rummaging through the piles, Oscar pressing buttons on everything he finds.

"This stuff is seriously old-school," Adjoa says, crouching as she reads out the names etched on the plastic casing. "*Altair 8800, Acorn Atom, Commodore 64.* These aren't computers. They're antiques."

"That's why nothing works," Oscar growls, flicking a switch on a chunky monitor from off to on. Its boxlike screen stays blank. "It's just electronic junk."

Glancing around, I try to find the door where we came in. There's no sign of it underneath the eaves behind us—only a bare brick wall. Turning back, I peer beyond the mounds of electronics into the gloom at the far end of the attic, but all I can see there is the shape of an old armchair, its back turned toward me. There's no door there either. And anyway, that isn't the way we came in.

The only door I *can* see is a trapdoor in the middle of the floor. Ibrahim is already crouching over it, twisting the latch to try to pull it open. He slowly shakes his head. "It's locked."

Standing next to me, Min scribbles in her notebook.

"Only one visible escape route," she mutters. "Locked."

"Don't worry," I say, reaching out to help Ibrahim back to his feet. "That's how these games work. We've got to solve the puzzles to find the way out."

"What puzzles?" Oscar snorts, breaking open a cardboard box and peering inside at the contents before shoving it to one side. "This isn't an escape room—it's more like a yard sale."

An avalanche of cassette tapes slide out from the tear that Oscar's made in the box, falling to the floor in a clatter of plastic.

"Everything is part of the game," Min says, glancing up from her notebook. "We've just got to work out what we need to do."

I look around the attic again. Beneath the light, the yellowing hard drives and dead computer screens stare back at me like tombstones. I don't want to agree with him, but I can't help feeling that Oscar's right. How are we supposed to figure out what we need to do when nothing works?

Ibrahim picks up the end of one of the computer cables. "Maybe we just need to plug this in?"

Oscar fixes him with a withering stare. "Find the plug, save the world," he says, his words dripping with sarcasm. "Yeah, I'm sure that'll work."

Adjoa turns on him angrily. "Well, what's your bright idea?" she asks, jabbing her finger in Oscar's direction. "This stuff's got to be here for a reason. If we can get it to work, it might give us a clue."

"We need to take this place apart," Oscar replies. "If there are any clues hidden among these piles of junk, that's the only way we're going to find them."

Adjoa narrows her eyes. "That's the stupidest idea I've ever heard."

"See if you can—"

"Can we just—"

"Give me the—"

Everyone starts talking at once. I stare at them in disbelief, my gaze flicking from Oscar to Adjoa, then to Ibrahim and Min, their voices getting louder and louder as they try to make themselves heard.

This is my team. We're supposed to work together to find the Answer.

We don't stand a chance.

I turn away. Dad said this game was going to be fun, but it's turning into a total headache.

Then, above their arguing voices, I catch a strange noise at the very edge of my hearing. A metallic clicking like a key being turned in a lock.

I glance down at the trapdoor, but the sound isn't coming from there.

"Hey," I say, trying to get everyone's attention. "Can you hear that?"

Nobody's listening, except to their own voices.

The clicking noise comes again and I look around, trying to work out exactly where it's coming from.

At first I think it might be one of the computers, but as I trace a path through the piles of out-of-date hardware, I realize that the sound is coming from the far end of the attic. I peer into the gloom, unable to see anything beyond the high back of the broad armchair.

I push on. Tiny specks of dust dance before my eyes, and the shadows lengthen around me now as I block out the light. The sound is getting louder too, like metallic teeth catching on a spinning gear. I shiver, the arguing voices behind me fading as I focus all my attention on finding out what is making this noise.

And then I see him: the man sitting motionless in the armchair. No, not exactly motionless. The white-gloved fingers of his right hand drum against the desk he's seated behind, the rhythmic clicks worming their way inside my mind. In the center of the desk a chessboard is set up for a game. My heart skips a beat as I glance up to meet the man's gaze, his dark-gray eyes staring into mine. He looks like the kind of magician you'd find in a book of old fairy tales. His beard is black and pointed, and there's a severe expression on his face. He's dressed in fire-red robes, the collar and sleeves trimmed with fur, while his dark features glower beneath a jeweled turban.

My eyes are drawn to a precious stone in the center. It looks like a black pearl pinned to the front of his turban, a red dot gleaming at the heart of this gem. I remember the camera lens I saw outside The Escape and hear an echo of the Host's words inside my mind: *I will be monitoring your every move.*

He's watching me now.

The man's fingers stop their drumming, and the silence that follows is even worse.

"Ami!" Adjoa calls out from the other side of the attic. "What've you found?"

"I think you need to see this," I say, keeping my eyes fixed on the camera lens. "All of you."

4

There's a scramble as the others rush to join me, all arguments forgotten as they crowd around the desk.

"What is this?" Oscar asks. He raps his knuckles on the table. "Hello? Is anybody home?"

The man doesn't move, his expression unchanged as he stares blankly ahead.

"It's the Chess Player of Maelzel," Min says, her dark eyes sparkling with delight. "An automaton that was built over two hundred and fifty years ago."

As soon as she says this, I breathe a sigh of relief. I didn't know at first if this man was real or not. Some of these escape rooms use actors to make the game seem more believable, but as I look more closely I can now see the sheen of his waxwork skin.

"You mean like a robot?" Adjoa asks.

"Kind of," Min replies. "An automaton was a machine that could imitate the actions of a living creature. There were mechanical birds and clockwork dancers—these early robots performed the same repetitive movements every time they were switched on—but the Chess Player of Maelzel was different. Its inventor claimed that his machine could defeat any human player at the game of chess."

With a clicking whirr, the man slowly moves his head from side to side, his deep-set eyes surveying the chessboard in front of him. I hold my breath, waiting to see what he does next. His left arm jerks forward, the movement so sudden that I take a step back in surprise. Fingers splayed, his hand descends to pick up a white pawn directly in front of his king, moving the piece two squares forward before setting the pawn down again. As his arm jerkily returns to its original position, I realize what we're supposed to do.

We have to play.

Leaning closer, I quickly slide a black pawn forward one square.

"Hey," Oscar says, raising his voice in protest. "Who said you could play the robot?"

I shoot him a look. "I'm a chess champion," I say, pointing to a pin on my top. On the front of this badge a gold knight stands proudly beneath the word GRANDMASTER. "Do you want to win this game or not?"

That shuts him up.

It was Dad who taught me chess. We used to play games that sometimes went on for days. The thing I like about it is that you have to follow the rules. Each player begins with the same sixteen pieces: eight pawns, two rooks, two knights, two bishops, one queen, and one king. And the goal is always the same—to attack your opponent's king until it can't escape. Checkmate.

But to get there you've got to be clever, figuring out the best way to attack your opponent's pieces while defending your own. It's a game that needs logic, strategy, and skill, and I'm pretty good at those things. That's why Dad stopped playing me in the end—I kept winning all the time.

The chess player whirrs to life once more, his left arm reaching out to pick up another pawn. As the clockwork gears click into position, he sets this pawn down alongside the first—a front line of soldiers advancing toward my army of black chess pieces. But before his arm even returns to its resting position, I slide another of my pawns forward to face his.

The clockwork man pauses for a moment, fingers trembling as his hand hovers above the board. I don't think he was expecting me to move so fast. His head slowly moves from side to side again. It looks like he's thinking, but I suspect this is just for show. Then his arm jerks back as he picks up a knight and moves it into play.

That's what I thought he was going to do.

I take his pawn.

First blood to me.

"Nice move," Adjoa says as I place the captured pawn on the table. I smile, but before I can start to feel too pleased with myself, the automaton strikes back.

With a clicking whirr I watch his gloved hand pick up the same knight again, this time transporting it sideways to capture my pawn.

"Yeah," Oscar says, patting me on the back as the man places my chess piece on his side of the desk. "Nice move, champ."

I ignore him, focusing on the board in front of me.

When you're playing chess, you need to look ahead, working out the moves you can make to improve your position. There are sixty-four squares on the board, and they give you so many possibilities. What I've got to do now is choose the right one.

Reaching out, I move one of my knights forward, but as his machinery whirrs the man does the same, so I move my other knight too.

"I don't know if this is what we're supposed to be doing," Min says, her voice urgent in my ear.

"What do you mean?" I ask, trying not to let myself get distracted as the clockwork man slides his bishop into play.

"The Chess Player of Maelzel was a fake," Min replies. "It wasn't a real machine. Whenever it played chess, there was someone hiding behind the scenes making the moves."

"You mean like *The Wizard of Oz?*" Adjoa asks. "I love that movie." She clicks the heels of her neon-green sneakers together. "*There's no place like home.*"

Keeping my eyes fixed on the chessboard, I move the pawn in front of my king forward one square. It's all going to plan, my strategy taking shape inside my mind.

"That's right," Min says as the chess player moves his second knight into play. "And it's only when Dorothy unmasks the real wizard that she's able to find her way home. Maybe that's what we need to do to find the Answer. We need to unmask the person who's controlling this machine."

I'm only half listening, keeping my attention on the game. I can see the moves I need to make unfolding one after another. I move my pawn to attack his first knight.

The chess player whirrs to life again, his left hand reaching out to pick up his knight. As the clockwork gears click, he moves the knight at a right angle to capture another of my pawns.

"He's winning," Oscar says.

I shake my head as I move my queen into play. "I don't think so."

Beneath his turban, the chess player rolls his lifeless eyes. If someone is controlling him like a puppet, it looks like they don't know what to do next.

His left arm slowly jerks across the board, first moving his king and then a rook as he castles. A defensive move, but he can't defend everything.

Smiling, I move one of my pawns forward, taking his knight.

Advantage: me.

I look around, waiting for the congratulations, but the others seem more interested in what Min's doing as she crouches at the front of the desk.

"The operator was usually hidden inside," she says, inspecting the doors and drawers there that hide its interior. "We just need to get these open somehow."

"I found this," Ibrahim says, holding up a small silver key. "It didn't fit the lock on the trapdoor, but maybe it'll work here."

There's a metallic clicking as the chess player slowly shakes his head, as if he's warning us about what we're about to do next.

Min tries the key in the lock on the front of the desk and I hear the same sound again.

"It works," Min says, glancing up with a grin. "Now let's see who the wizard really is."

We all crowd around as she opens the doors, revealing what's hidden inside the desk.

There's nothing there. No clockwork cogs and gears, no hidden machinery. No sign of a puppet master pulling the chess player's strings. The space beneath the desk is completely empty. All I can see through a grille at the back are the automaton's fire-red robes.

"I don't understand," Min says.

A whirring draws my eyes back to the chess player. His left arm is jerking forward again; his fingers close around his bishop, and he moves it diagonally to attack my king. As he sets the piece down, I hear a single word escape his lips.

"Check."

His voice sounds strangely human as I stare in disbelief at

the board. I didn't see this coming. I didn't even think I was under attack. Leaning forward, I quickly move my king out of check.

The whirring of machinery starts again, and I watch as the man moves his second bishop into play. I gaze up into his eyes, the sheen of his waxwork features glistening in the gloom. Are we sure he isn't real?

Feeling flustered, I move one of my pawns forward two spaces. You're allowed to do this when it's the first move your pawn makes, although Dad sometimes forgets this and accuses me of cheating.

The automaton moves his pawn too, putting me under attack.

Everyone's talking at once—offering me advice, suggesting tactics—but I just need to think.

I move my bishop diagonally one square, playing for time.

The clockwork clicking starts again, but I know there's no machinery to make this noise. It's a fake—just like Min said it was. A trick to distract us. The chess player's arm slowly jerks across the board, moving his rook one square to the left. But maybe the trick was to make us *think* it's not real?

There's no wizard to unmask, only a machine to beat. And that means I've got to win.

I move my knight to attack his bishop and then watch as he moves it back out of range. I move my king. He takes my pawn, so I take his in return. Everyone's silent as they watch the game unfold, the chess pieces dancing around the board: queen, bishop, bishop, rook. And that's when it all goes wrong.

From out of nowhere his rook storms the length of the board, capturing my queen. I stare at his gloved hand, dumbfounded, as it transports my piece to the edge, dropping it with a clunk on his side of the desk.

I'm in deep trouble now.

The queen is the most powerful piece in the game. She can move anywhere on the board, in every direction, any number of squares. If you lose your queen, winning becomes *so* much harder.

With a rush of frustration I move my bishop to take his rook, but this retaliation doesn't make me feel much better. With a clicking whirr, another white pawn is pushed forward, the chess player marshalling his pieces in a relentless attack.

I move my own pawns forward, but every move I make just feels like I'm staving off the inevitable. This machine is going to win.

Then Oscar reaches over me. Picking up one of my black knights, he jumps it forward two squares to take the chess player's queen.

"What are you doing?" I ask as he deposits this stolen piece on my side of the board. "Knights can only move in an L shape—not straight ahead."

"We can cheat," Oscar says, tipping a wink in the direction of my opponent. "Old Clocky here won't know any different."

With a metallic snick, the chess player roughly shakes his head. The white glove of his right hand raps against the desk three times, before he reaches out with his left to replace his white queen back in the position it was stolen from.

"I think he does."

Then the chess player makes his own move, advancing his rook threateningly. I don't know what to do and push my pieces around the board as I react to his probing attacks. It feels like I'm running out of time, his movements sounding like the ticking of a clock. I stare at the pieces that are left on the board, trying to see a way to win.

Near the far corner, one lonely black pawn has almost reached the other side. And as I look at this piece, I remember. The pawn might be the least powerful piece in the game, but when it reaches the end of the board it can change.

I push the pawn forward one square, then, in the same action, reach out to swap it for my queen. With a smile I nod toward the opposite corner, where the white king is now trapped, defenseless.

"Checkmate."

The man moves his head from side to side, his dark-gray eyes studying the chessboard in front of him. There's no way out. No move he can make to avoid checkmate. We've won.

He lifts his right arm, and for a second, I think he's going to shake my hand. Then his arm sweeps out in a rage, knocking all the pieces off the board and sending them flying.

Overhead, the lights turn red as a siren begins to blare.

"Ami!" Adjoa calls out. "What's happening?"

I look around the attic, the dead computer screens now blinking to life. Streams of letters and numbers scroll across their displays, the same message repeated again and again.

SELF-DESTRUCT SEQUENCE INITIATED

And then the numbers start to count down.

I turn toward the others to see their eyes wide with fear.

"I don't think we were supposed to win."

5

I can't think—my vision is flashing red as the siren blare seems to drown out everything. The others stand there, frozen in shock—all except one.

Ignoring the incessant sound, Min starts to carefully place the scattered chess pieces back in their starting positions, the rows of black and white pawns lining up against each other once more.

"What are you doing?" I ask, my heart hammering in my chest as the bulb overhead pulses with its crimson light.

Picking up a white knight from where it's fallen, Min leans across the chessboard to return it to its starting square.

"We need to play him again," she says, glancing up to meet the chess player's dark-eyed gaze. "Let him win and make this stop."

But as this last word escapes Min's lips, she suddenly drops the carved horse with a cry of alarm.

The chessboard is on fire, every square blazing with a

hissing flame. I don't know how this can be happening. There must be burners hidden beneath the desk somewhere and someone has turned the gas on. Draped over the edge of the board, the chess player's robes ignite, and Min recoils as the leaping flames lick at her sleeve. Quickly I drag Min back, beating away the flames as the automaton is set ablaze.

As he burns, I hear a mechanical clicking. The chess player is raising an arm to point his gloved finger directly at me. Through the flames I see his waxen face start to melt, but his dark eyes burn with a triumphant glare.

"Checkmate," he says, his teeth now bared in a snarl.

I look around, desperate to find something to put the fire out. Snapping into action, Ibrahim drags a dusty sheet off a stack of ancient computer equipment, revealing a row of cracked screens. But when he flings this sheet forward to smother the flames, it catches fire instead, spreading the blaze across the attic with a whiplash crackle. The scorching heat is so fierce that it forces us back. My eyes flick between the melting face of the automaton and the message that flashes from every computer screen:

SELF-DESTRUCT SEQUENCE INITIATED
98 . . . 97 . . . 96 . . . 95 . . .

My mind races as I try to understand what's gone wrong. This is The Escape. It's supposed to be an adventure, but as the attic burns, it doesn't feel like a game anymore.

From the heart of the flames I hear the chess player laugh. He still looks like some kind of magician, but this spell that he's cast is taking us straight to hell. The jeweled turban has slipped from his head, exposing a melting skull, but the pinned black pearl still gleams red. This must mean the camera's still filming. The Host can see what's going on.

"Something's gone wrong!" I shout, screaming straight into the camera lens. "You've got to let us out!"

But the chess player just grins as the flames consume him.

"Come on, Ami!" Ibrahim yells, pulling my arm to drag me away. Reluctantly I follow his lead, threading my way through the piles of electronic junk as the fire takes hold. On the other side of the attic, Min is already crouching over the hatch. I can see scorch marks on the sleeve of her denim jacket as she strains to pull the trapdoor open.

"It's no use," she says, meeting my gaze. "It's still locked!" Beneath the dark line of her bangs, I glimpse a flicker of fear darting across her face. "We must have missed something."

The siren is still screaming in my ear as I look around, trying to work out what that could be. Black smoke streams across the ceiling, the acrid taste making me choke. The far end of the attic is now an inferno. Bright-orange flames lick at the stacked computer monitors, the flickering numbers on their screens counting down as the plastic bubbles and burns.

73 . . . 72 . . . 71 . . . 70 . . .

Turning away from the spreading flames, I see Adjoa standing in front of a chunky desktop computer that looks like it escaped from the 1980s. Its green screen shows the same numbers counting down.

66 . . . 65 . . . 64 . . . 63 . . .

"What are you doing?" I ask as she frantically taps at its keys.

"I'm trying to stop the countdown," she says, her fingers clacking across the keyboard without pause. "I need to hack the code to find a way in, but nothing's working so far."

I'm just about to ask what I can do to help, when Oscar pushes in front of me. He grabs hold of the computer before ripping the keyboard away from Adjoa.

"There's no time to find a way in," he shouts as he throws the whole thing on the floor. "We've got to find a way out."

The monitor explodes as it hits the ground.

"You idiot!" Adjoa shouts back, turning toward him in fury. "What do you think you're doing?"

"What we should've done from the start," Oscar replies, crunching his sneaker down on the keyboard. Its casing cracks, spitting keys across the floor. "Taking this place apart."

I stare at him in disbelief. Oscar seems to think that smashing things up will help us escape, but the numbers scrolling across the countless computer screens behind him tell a different story. Through the haze, I count them down.

What happens when they reach zero?

As Oscar and Adjoa continue to bicker, I glance back at the searing brightness of the fire. It looks like it's alive, the crackling sheets of flame leaping from floor to ceiling as they engulf the stacks of computer equipment. Every breath I take burns the back of my throat, the billowing smoke hiding the rest of the attic from view. I want to run, but there's no way out.

"We need to find an extinguisher!" I yell over Oscar's and Adjoa's bickering voices. "We've got to put this fire out!"

Close by, the walnut casing of a vintage computer system bursts into flames. The sudden heat is so intense I have to turn away. I catch sight of Ibrahim, his head bent as he rummages through the toppling boxes of tech. Wires and cables spill to the floor, circuit boards scattering as he searches for something to save our lives.

"Look at this!" he shouts, turning to face me.

I'm desperately hoping to see a fire extinguisher, but all he's holding is what looks like some kind of handheld game console, and its gray plastic case doesn't make it look like much fun.

"What is it?" I ask as Min crowds around too.

"It's a chess computer," Ibrahim says, holding the device out toward me. "And it's playing your game."

Two sets of rubber-coated buttons flank a gray-and-green LCD screen, the name of the handheld console written above it in faded red letters.

As I take hold of the device, I see chess pieces flickering across its pixelated screen, the moves that they're making eerily familiar. White pawn to D4, black pawn to D5, white knight to C3, black pawn takes white. Ibrahim is right—this is the game I played when I beat the automaton, the match that lit the fire that's burning the attic down.

Standing at my shoulder, Min gasps in excitement.

"You can play the game again," she says as black and white knights flicker across the board.

I nod, my eyes flicking over the game's controls. LAST PIECE, LAST MOVE, NEXT PIECE, NEXT MOVE. I press down on the D-pad to try to select the next piece.

"But this time I can make sure I lose."

My finger flicks to the NEXT MOVE button, trying to force my king into play, but instead I see my bishop slide across the board. This is the exact same move I made before. I push hard on the buttons, but nothing seems to work. It's like the computer won't let me play. I watch the pieces dart across the screen, every move preordained. I know how this game ends, and there's nothing I can do to stop it.

"It's no use," I say, glancing up to meet Min's gaze. Her dark eyes shine with the same fear that haunts mine. "It won't let me change the past."

Behind Min, a teetering stack of computer equipment collapses with a crash. Oscar is still tearing the place apart while

Adjoa screams at him to stop. Sweat drips from Ibrahim's face as he stares in horror at the solid wall of flames bearing down on us. Through wreaths of smoke, I can see the melting plastic machinery, the relentless countdown continuing across every splintered screen.

33 . . . 32 . . . 31 . . . 30 . . .

I can't think. I can't breathe. Dad said this was a game, but it feels like the end of everything.

"There must be something we're missing," Ibrahim shouts, his voice strained above the roar of the flames. "We're looking at this the wrong way."

I glance down at the e-CHESS 2000, the same game still playing over and over again. The game controls are on the right, but along the left-hand side of the screen are four more buttons: SETUP, SHIFT, HINT, ESC. Ibrahim says there's something we're missing. We just need a clue to work out what it is.

I jab my thumb down on the HINT key and watch as a message starts to scroll across the game's LCD screen.

FIND THE ANSWER. SAVE THE WORLD.
FIND THE ANSWER. SAVE THE WORLD.

As the message scrolls, I can still see the black and white pieces moving across the digital chessboard. The game won't stop playing, and this hint doesn't help. We already know we're supposed to save the world, but right now we just need to save ourselves.

"Keep trying," Min says as Oscar scrambles toward the hatch.

I jab my thumb against the button again and watch the message change.

THE CLOCK IS TICKING.
THE COUNTDOWN HAS BEGUN.

That's what the Host told us before we stepped into this place. I glance up to see the fire all around us now, the scrolling numbers still counting down as the screens melt.

14 . . . 13 . . . 12 . . . 11 . . .

There's no time left. There's no way out.

"Ami!" Adjoa shouts, her voice frantic amid the flames. "Do something!"

I press the HINT key again, but the message stays the same. It's like the Host is mocking us now. I rack my brains, trying to figure out what to do next, but all I hear are his words rattling around inside my head.

The clock is ticking—the countdown has begun. Everything is part of the game. All you need to succeed is hidden inside The Escape.

Oscar pounds on the locked hatch as the numbers count down.

10 . . . 9 . . . 8 . . . 7 . . .

I stare at the chess machine, my gaze flicking across its buttons as I search for what we've missed. And then I see it.

ESC

Escape.

The answer is staring me in the face. *All you need to succeed is hidden inside The Escape.*

5 . . . 4 . . . 3 . . . 2 . . .

I jab down hard on the ESC key, feeling the rubber squish beneath my thumb.

The siren blare suddenly cuts to silence, and then I hear a loud clanking noise.

"It's opening!" Oscar shouts, lifting the trapdoor hatch as we hear a grating, slithering sound like a giant metallic snake. We all crowd around the hatch, peering down into the darkness as Oscar lowers himself over the edge.

"There's a ladder," he says, his head and shoulders slowly vanishing as he starts to descend. As soon as Oscar's head is clear, Min lowers herself over the edge, the clatter of her steps ringing out as she disappears too. Ibrahim's next, with Adjoa following close behind.

I look around. Everything's burning. I'm still holding the e-CHESS 2000, its LCD screen now frozen in a stalemate.

"Come on, Ami!"

At Adjoa's shout, I toss the computer into the flames. Then, lowering myself onto the ladder, I pull the hatch closed over my head and start climbing down into the darkness.

6

Beneath my fingers, the metal feels greasy as I reach from rung to rung, my foot slipping as I take another step down. I can't see a thing as I descend; the darkness that surrounds me is absolute.

Nobody's said a word since we left the burning attic behind. The only thing that tells me I'm not alone in the dark is the clatter of footsteps I can hear beneath me, their juddering vibrations making the ladder sway back and forth.

It feels like we've been climbing down forever.

Peering into the inky blackness, I think I can see a faint glimmer of light below. This dimness starts to lighten as I scramble down the rungs, a glowing circle of light pooling at the base of the ladder. I can see the others clustered around it: Oscar, Adjoa, Ibrahim, and Min, their faces peering up as I clamber down the last few rungs.

The ladder doesn't quite reach the ground, so I have to jump the final stretch. A cloud of dust rises as my feet hit the floor and I sink to my knees, the thud of my landing echoing into the darkness.

"You made it," Adjoa says, smiling with relief as she reaches out a hand to help me up. "We all got out of there."

But before I can even open my mouth to reply, a harsh clanking drowns out everything else. The noise is coming from directly overhead: the metal ladder is being wound back up again, its rungs disappearing into the darkness.

I look at the others. We might have escaped the fire, but as I try to peer beyond the circle of light that surrounds us, I don't know what we're supposed to do next.

"Where are we?" Oscar growls. "I can't see a thing down here."

As if in reply to his question, the light brightens, pushing back against the gloom to reveal exactly where we are.

"Oh, wow," I breathe.

We're in some kind of library, but one bigger than I've ever seen in my life. A labyrinth of shelves stretches out in every direction: dark wooden stacks that reach from floor to ceiling, all lined with endless rows of books. I can't see where the light is coming from, and as I crane my neck to peer into the heights of the nearest stack, I realize I can't even see the ceiling. The silent shelves seem to stretch into infinity. It looks like the books go on forever.

As I glance back at the others, I catch Min's gaze and see the hint of a smile creeping across her lips.

"Well, it looks like we've come to the right place," she says, walking toward a large hexagonal desk that stands at the center of the stacks. It reminds me in a strange way of the reception desk I saw when I first entered The Escape. But where the lines of that low round desk were clean and white, this dark wooden desk stands chest high, its six sides covered in a layer of grime.

"What do you mean?" Oscar snaps. He kicks up clouds of dust as he follows Min toward the central desk. "That electronic junkyard upstairs was more interesting than a stupid library. I want some action and adventure, not a bedtime story."

"Don't you see?" Min says, gesturing toward the groaning bookshelves. "Whatever the question is, we'll find the Answer in the library. We just need to find the right book."

I look around at the cavernous stacks. Staring down the nearest aisle of shelves, I can't even see where they come to an end. And there are dozens of these gloomy passageways stretching to all points of the compass. There must be hundreds of thousands of books in this place. Millions, maybe . . .

"And it looks like we're expected," Ibrahim calls out, reaching across the dusty desk to pick up a handful of cards. He offers one to each of us in turn, and taking mine, I look down to see my name in bright white letters against a jet-black background.

"Why'd you give me this?" Oscar asks, strumming his black plastic card against his fingertips.

"It's your library card," Ibrahim explains, holding up his own so we can see we've all got the same. "Bibliothèque Universelle—the Universal Library. If we're supposed to find a book, then maybe these will help us."

"I don't need a stupid library card," Oscar replies, shoving his into the pocket of his zipped top. "We don't even know if we're looking for a book. There might be a secret passage or something hidden in this place. We just need to start exploring."

Turning from the desk, Oscar strides toward the nearest stack, his sneakers kicking up fresh clouds of dust.

"Who's coming with me?" he calls.

Glancing at the others, I see Adjoa roll her eyes. It doesn't look like Oscar has learned anything from the mess we made upstairs. One of Dad's catchphrases pops into my head, the one he always says whenever he's trying to teach me something and I treat it like a race and end up making a mistake.

Fools rush in where angels fear to tread.

And now I know what he means.

"Wait a second!" I call, stopping Oscar in his tracks. "We need to figure out a plan first before we make any more mistakes."

"And whose fault is that?" Oscar snaps, turning toward me with a sneer. "It was your mistake that turned that chess player into a Roman candle."

"That's what I mean," I say, trying to hide my annoyance at the way Oscar's pinning all the blame on me. "We thought we were doing the right thing, but by rushing to play the game, we messed things up. We only just got out of that room alive."

"When you're playing an escape game, everything can be a clue," Min says, backing me up. "These library cards have our names on them. They must mean something."

I glance down at mine again, turning the card over in my hand. There's a barcode on the back, the strip of black parallel lines framed in a white panel. My mind races. Barcodes are used to store information. Maybe the clue we need is hidden inside these parallel lines.

"Have you seen this?" I say, holding up my card to show the others. "If we're supposed to use these cards, then we need to find a card reader."

My gaze flicks back to the imposing desk. There's no librarian to help us. No sign either of any of the computers they use to check out books. Just a thick layer of dust showing that nobody's been in this place for years.

"Over here!"

Adjoa's shout makes me spin around. She's heading in the opposite direction from Oscar, marching toward another long avenue of books. But as I watch, Adjoa stops at what looks like a signpost that's half hidden in the shadows cast by the towering stack.

We race over to see what she's found, dust swirling beneath our feet as we reach the signpost.

At least, I thought it was a signpost, but close up I realize it's attached to some kind of information point. A black metal column rises from a broad circular base. It reaches about three meters tall, spindly cylindrical arms branching off near the top to point in different directions. My eyes are drawn to the display halfway up the pillar, at the height of my head. As the others crowd around the machine, I peer over Adjoa's shoulder to read the message on the curved screen.

WELCOME TO THE LIBRARY
PLEASE SCAN YOUR CARD

Adjoa places her library card in the empty space directly below the display. I watch as the thin red line of a laser beam slithers across the barcode on the back of the card, and then I see the message on the screen change.

WELCOME, ADJOA
YOU HAVE ONE RESERVATION
PLEASE HEAD TO YOUR COLLECTION POINT

Above my head, I hear a whirring, and glancing up, I see one of the cylindrical arms spinning around. It comes to a sudden stop, the spindly finger on the end of the pole now pointing down one of the nearest avenues of shelves. At the end of this stack, a brass lantern glimmers to life, the light it casts illuminating a sign that reads THIS WAY TO COLLECTION POINT A.

Adjoa grins.

"That's A for Adjoa," she says, pocketing her library card and turning to face the rest of us. "Well, I know where I've got to go. You need to scan your cards too to see if this gives us any more clues."

I'm the closest to the machine, but before I can even get my card ready, Oscar barges ahead of me.

"Get out of the way," he snaps, shouldering me to one side as he scans his card. "If we need a stupid book to find the Answer, then I'm going to be the first one to find it."

A new welcome message appears on the screen as, with a whirr, another metallic arm above our heads starts to turn.

WELCOME, OSCAR
YOU HAVE ONE RESERVATION
PLEASE HEAD TO YOUR COLLECTION POINT

When it comes to a stop, the arm is pointing in the opposite direction. I turn around to see a lantern now shining at the entrance to another long avenue of books. Beneath its glow, I can just make out some words, written in gold: THIS WAY TO COLLECTION POINT O.

"It's the same way I was going before," Oscar grunts, flashing me a look. "Told you I had the right idea."

I stare at him, dumbfounded. If it wasn't for me, Oscar wouldn't even know he was looking for a book. While I'm still thinking of a sarcastic comeback, Ibrahim and Min take it in turns to scan their cards. The message on the screen tells them both the same thing.

YOU HAVE ONE RESERVATION
PLEASE HEAD TO YOUR COLLECTION POINT

The metallic arms slowly revolve, pointing Ibrahim one way and Min the other. I realize now why I thought this information point was a signpost at first: its cylindrical poles point to the four corners of the library. It's like whoever made these reservations wants to split us up.

"Go on, Ami," Adjoa says. "It's your turn now."

Placing my card into position, I watch the laser beam scroll across the barcode, then look up to see the fresh message on the screen.

WELCOME, AMI
YOU HAVE 129,864,880 OVERDUE BOOKS
YOUR ACCOUNT HAS BEEN SUSPENDED

This can't be right.

I scan the card again, thinking the machine must have made some kind of mistake, but the message stays the same.

Leaning over my shoulder, Adjoa lets out a low whistle. "That's going to be a *monumental* fine."

I don't understand. I've never been to this library before, let alone borrowed millions of books. This doesn't make any sense. It's impossible.

I take my library card from under the scanner and rub the barcode on the back of my sleeve. Maybe there's a speck of dust on it that's made the reader go haywire. I place the card back in the empty space below the screen and watch as the thin red line of the laser rolls across the barcode again.

Nothing changes. This machine still thinks I've borrowed almost 130 million books and they're all overdue.

"Well, I don't have time to hang around with you losers," Oscar says, striding toward the stacks. "I've got the Answer to find, and I'll be back here before you've even figured out what the question is."

We watch him go, his sneakers leaving prints in the dust as he heads down the lantern-lit passage of books.

Min turns to the rest of us. "Oscar's right," she says. "We need to collect our reservations."

Ibrahim nods, but I feel my face flushing red.

It's not fair. Everyone else has a mission—a reservation to collect from somewhere inside this Universal Library—but my account's been suspended. How am I supposed to find the Answer if I can't even play the game?

"Don't worry, Ami," Adjoa says, sensing my disappointment. "You can come with me. I could use some help finding my way in this place."

Her mouth curves into a smile as I nod gratefully.

I know she's only saying it to be nice, but I can't help feeling kind of relieved that I'm not going to be left on my own. There's something a tiny bit creepy about this deserted library.

"We'll meet back here as soon as we've found the reservations," Ibrahim says, still holding on to his library card. "I know Oscar thinks he's going to find the Answer on his own, but there must be a reason we've all got our own cards."

I glance back at the information point; my Account Suspended message is still displayed on the screen. I don't know how this fits into Ibrahim's theory. Maybe it's the Host's way of letting me know he doesn't like the way I play.

Raising my chin, I look to where the brass lantern lights the way to Collection Point A. As Ibrahim and Min set off in opposite directions, Adjoa and I start walking toward our own aisle in this vast cathedral of books.

It's time to explore the library.

7

"What do you think of the others?" Adjoa asks, our footsteps echoing as we walk along the gloomy corridor of books.

Motes of dust dance in the eerie glow cast by the lanterns fixed at the end of each gallery of shelves. Each lantern only flickers into life when we reach the start of the next row. It's as if the library doesn't want us to see what lies ahead.

"I don't know," I say, feeling distracted by Adjoa's question as I strain my eyes against the gloom. "What do *you* think of them?"

"I like Ibrahim," Adjoa replies without missing a beat. "I like the way he looks at things. The way he found that chess computer and the library cards too. You need someone like him on your team. A *finder*. Someone who can see the things that everyone else has missed."

I nod my head. What Adjoa's saying makes sense. If it hadn't been for Ibrahim's spotting skills, we'd still be stuck in that burning attic. At the back of my neck I feel my skin start to prickle as I remember the roar of the flames. I still can't believe that the Host nearly turned us into toast.

"Min's the clever one," Adjoa continues, counting off the others on the fingers of her left hand. "Just look at the way she knew all about that Chess Player of Marzipan or whatever it was called. She's always scribbling things down in that notebook of hers. If you ask me, she's the brains of this team."

I can't help feeling a bit miffed that Adjoa thinks Min's cleverer than me. After all, *I* was the one who worked out that we needed to press the ESCAPE key to get out of the attic. But there's no point in reminding Adjoa of this, as she's already moved on to letting me know what she thinks of Oscar.

"We're just unlucky we've ended up with someone like *him*," she says. The way she spits out this last word makes it perfectly clear who she's talking about. "In an escape room some players are good at finding clues, others are skilled at solving puzzles, but some people just like to move fast and break things. That's what Oscar does. He's your classic *destroyer*. He'll use brute force rather than brains every time. We'll just have to try to keep him on a short leash to stop him from wrecking the game for the rest of us."

The next lantern flickers into life, illuminating the galleries ahead, which look just like all the rest. A sliding ladder is fastened close to the wall, its wooden rungs offering access to the out-of-reach shelves, but as I glance up into the heights of the stack, I don't think anyone would dare to climb to the top.

"What about me?" I ask, turning my gaze back toward Adjoa. "What do I bring to the team?"

Folding her arms across her chest, Adjoa makes a show of sizing me up.

"A bit of everything, I think. You're clever like Min, good at spotting things just like Ibrahim, and you're not scared to stand up to Oscar." A mischievous smile creeps across her lips. "I reckon that makes you team captain."

I feel myself blush, a sudden warmth blooming across my cheeks.

"No, thanks," I say, brushing Adjoa's compliments away with a shake of my head. "We don't need a team captain."

Adjoa looks like she's ready to argue the point, so I quickly change the subject by throwing the question back at her.

"How about you?" I ask as another brass lantern flickers to life to light the path ahead. "What are your special skills?"

"Me?" Adjoa grins. "I'm this team's secret weapon. Think Lara Croft meets Indiana Jones, but with a better sense of style. Deadly pit with snakes in it? No problem. Falling swords and rolling boulders? Bring them on. Booby-trapped statue? Just give me a shout. I'm a natural-born adventurer. This game was made for me.

"Come on," she says, quickening her step as we continue our trek down the avenue of books. "We don't want the others to beat us to all the fun stuff."

It's strange to think of the others, somewhere in this library, all searching for the same thing. As Adjoa hurries ahead, I trail my finger along one of the shelves, skimming over the leather-bound spines that sit there tightly packed. A musty smell hangs in the air, the scent making me feel as if I'm breathing in the books themselves. In the glow from the lantern I read the titles on the spines, each one picked out in golden letters: *Do Glaciers Listen? Can a Submarine Swim? Why Don't Things Fall Down?* We're supposed to be looking for the Answer, but all I can see here are stupid questions.

Pausing for a second, I take one of the books down from the shelf. Its red-leather binding is scuffed with age, but at least the cracked letters of its title aren't asking another question.

EXPRESSION OF THE EMOTIONS
by Charles Darwin

It looks like one of those old-fashioned books that Dad's always trying to get me to read. Ones that he thinks will improve my mind. Like that time he gave me the complete works of William Shakespeare and then got annoyed when he caught me reading a walkthrough for *The Legend of Zelda*. He says I need to broaden my horizons, but I don't see why I can't do that in a video game.

As I flick through its pages, the book falls open at a photograph: a sepia-tinged picture of a baby, her eyes screwed up and her mouth open wide. It looks like she's crying, her face captured mid-scream, but as I stare at the picture I start to think that maybe she's laughing instead.

It's like two opposite emotions are captured in the same photograph. The expressions look so similar to me. The baby screams, but is it with joy or despair? Absentmindedly I brush my fingertip across the photograph and gasp as I feel a teardrop rolling down the page.

I stare at the baby, dumbfounded, trying to work out if this is real, and then I see a line of text appearing beneath the picture. . . .

Do you know how it feels to feel, Ami?

I slam the book shut, sending a fresh shower of dust to the floor. The words were printed on the page, but it was like I could hear them in my head. It sounded like the Host himself, whispering in my ear.

"Ami!"

Adjoa's shout pulls me out of my fear. Quickly sliding the book back onto the shelf, I turn to see her some twenty meters ahead. She's standing directly beneath another brass-bound lantern, the eerie light it casts showing me a solid wall of empty shelves.

It's a dead end.

Thinking we've come the wrong way, I feel my heart start to sink, but then Adjoa steps to one side to reveal a sign.

WELCOME TO COLLECTION POINT A

"We're here," she says.

8

"But where's the book?" I ask, desperately searching the shelves for any sign of the reservation that should be waiting for us.

"I don't know," Adjoa replies, her hands and knees grimed with dust as she climbs to her feet after checking the bottom shelf. "It must be here somewhere."

I look over my shoulder. The towering stacks that lined our path are shrouded in darkness again. The only light still shining comes from the lantern above the sign welcoming us to Collection Point A. But as I turn back to inspect the empty shelves that mark the end of this blind alley, I still can't see anything for us to collect.

"Maybe the library machine got it wrong," I say, remembering the millions of overdue books it said I'd borrowed. "Maybe this isn't where we were supposed to go."

Lifting her gaze, Adjoa peers up at the countless shelves that stretch out of reach.

"We haven't looked everywhere yet."

Another sliding ladder rests at the far end of this empty bookcase, but as I wait for Adjoa to spring into action, she turns to me instead.

"Can you find it, Ami?"

She's holding out her library card for me to take.

I shake my head, thinking that she's just trying to be nice to me again.

"It's your reservation," I say, gently pushing her hand away. "Not mine. You should be the one to find it."

But Adjoa seems to wince at my refusal, a pained look flitting across her face. She casts a nervous glance toward the ladder, its wooden rungs covered in a thin layer of dust.

"I—I can't," she says, stuttering out her reply. "I just can't."

I feel confused. Until now, Adjoa's been the one leading the way, but she seems to have frozen on me. And then she tells me why.

"I'm scared of heights."

I look at her sideways. "How can you be scared of heights?" I ask, struggling to hide my incredulity. "You climbed down that ladder from the attic, and that felt like it was a mile high."

"That was different," Adjoa says, pouting slightly. "I couldn't see where I was in the dark." She glances up again at the endless shelves, all lit by an eerie glow. "Not like now."

Holding out her card again, she meets my gaze plaintively. "Please, Ami. Find it for me."

Adjoa said she was a natural-born adventurer, just like

Indiana Jones, but it looks like her secret fear is heights, not snakes.

Taking the library card, I slip it into my pocket, next to mine.

"Okay," I say, reaching for the ladder. "But there's no guarantee I'll find anything up there. This might just be a red herring."

"Thanks, skipper," Adjoa says, a relieved smile breaking across her face. "I owe you one."

The rungs creak in protest as I start to climb.

"I'll hold the ladder," she says, stationing herself at the bottom as soon as my legs are clear. "Don't worry about it coming away from the wall."

"I wasn't," I mutter as I reach for the next rung. "Not until you mentioned it."

A sheer wall of shelf edges stretches toward the ceiling. Just as with all the other stacks, I can't see where this one ends; the highest of the ledges disappears into the darkness. The ladder seems to tremble as I hoist myself up to the next rung.

That's the thing about fear. It's infectious.

Lowering my gaze, I hold on to the ladder a little more tightly as I peer along the length of the shelf straight ahead. There's no need to look up or down; I can just keep my eyes fixed in front of me, searching one shelf at a time as I climb. But every dusty shelf that I peer down is empty; there's no sign anywhere of Adjoa's reservation.

Dust sticks to my fingers as I go higher and higher. It

doesn't look like anyone has been up this ladder for years, so how can a reservation be waiting for us here?

"I can't see anything," I shout, half hoping that Adjoa will just say to give up.

No such luck.

"Keep on looking," she calls, her voice sounding farther away than I thought it would be. "Remember, everything could be part of the game. Even these empty shelves could be hiding a secret. I know you'll find something, Ami. I can feel it in my bones."

A bead of sweat forms on my brow as I hear this echo of the Host. *Everything is part of the game.* I remember the book that I found with the picture of the baby whose tear seemed to run down the page. The words I read there whisper again inside my brain. *Do you know how it feels to feel, Ami?*

I nod as I keep climbing. I feel scared.

The Host said he'd be monitoring our every move. But in the first room of this game he almost left us to die in the flames. The ladder shakes as I reach for the next rung. If he's watching now, will he catch me if I fall?

I don't dare look down to see how far I've climbed. I just keep searching, one shelf at a time. Some shelves are labeled with a single word scribbled inside a brass holder fixed to the edge: ZOOLOGY, PHILOSOPHY, SCIENCE, HISTORY, and more. All human knowledge, classified and organized in the library. Min thought we'd find the Answer here, but each label I see catalogs only a thick layer of dust. The shelves are empty.

Pausing for a second, I glance up to see how far I've got left to climb. The stack stretches into the darkness, the sheer wall of shelves looking just as steep as before. My heart sinks. What's the point of climbing if I never reach the top?

Then I see it, a slim volume lying on its side, nearly pushed out of sight in a dark corner of the shelf. Keeping a tight grip on the ladder with one hand, I reach across to pick up the book. It's covered in a thick layer of dust, but, as I brush this off, I can read the title etched, in golden-green letters, on its cover.

A Natural Treasury

A buzz of excitement starts to thrum through my brain. This must be it.

I know I should head down the ladder right away to show Adjoa what I've found. It's her reservation, after all. But I can't resist opening the book to see what it's about. In the gloom of the shelf I can just make out these jagged lines:

> There is another sky,
> Ever serene and fair,
> And there is another sunshine,
> Though it be darkness there;

Never mind faded forests,
Never mind silent fields—
Here is a little forest,
Whose leaf is ever green . . .

But as I try to read the remaining lines, the words seem to slip from the page. I watch astounded as the black ink turns to dust, and as I let out a gasp of surprise, these specks are blown into the air. I stare down at the book, the page now a blank sheet of whiteness.

Feeling sick, I start to flick through the book, thinking that somehow I've made a mistake. But every page just spills out a fresh fountain of dust and, as I strain my eyes against the gloom, I see they're *all* blank now.

I don't know how this can be happening, but as I rack my brain for an explanation, I notice that it seems much darker than before. I look up, trying to work out why, and feel the fear rise in my throat.

Darkness seems to be falling out of the sky, but then I realize.

It's not darkness. It's dust.

9

"Did you find it?" Adjoa asks, her eager voice bubbling in my ear as soon as my feet hit the floor.

Turning around, I reach for the book in my pocket, my knuckles still white from gripping the ladder.

"I found this," I tell her, handing over the slim leather-bound text.

Adjoa starts to flip through the book, her excited smile undimmed by the gloom. But as she turns the pages, this smile starts to fade before she stops to look up at me with a questioning gaze.

"It's blank," she says, a puzzled frown furrowing her brow. "There's nothing written inside."

My heart thuds in my chest. "There was something," I say, struggling to explain exactly what I saw. "It was a poem, I think. But as I read it, the words just turned into dust. Every page was the same. It was like the book was being erased."

Even as I speak it seems to be getting darker. Reaching out,

I hold out my hand and watch the dust landing there. Each speck seems to gleam in the glow cast by the lantern light and, as I glance up, I see the dust still falling like rain. Where's this coming from?

A terrible thought creeps into my head. Turning away, I head toward the darkened stacks; their tightly packed shelves are a stark contrast to the empty dead end of Collection Point A. With a mounting sense of dread I pull out a handful of books and watch them spill across the floor. Across scuffed leather covers, the gilt letters of their titles seem to spell out a message to me: *What Have We Done; Our Final Warning; This Changes Everything.*

"What are you doing?" Adjoa calls.

But as I crouch to flip through their pages, my answer sticks in my throat. Swirls of soot rise like mist from the books. Blinking, I cough, waving my hand to clear the air, but when I look down, the pages are blank. There are no words left, only dust.

A shadow falls and I look up to see Adjoa standing over me. Her smile has vanished, and I see in her eyes the same look of fear that I feel inside.

"Something bad is happening here," I say, clambering to my feet. "We've got to get back."

We start to run, retracing our steps along this dark avenue of books. One by one, the brass lanterns flicker to life as we pass, but the light they cast now seems shrouded by shadows.

Black specks dance in front of my eyes as I see the footprints we left slowly disappearing beneath a curtain of dust. I pull the neck of my T-shirt up, covering my mouth and nose.

"Maybe this is coming from the fire in the attic," Adjoa says, spluttering for breath as we run.

I shake my head, finding it hard to breathe too. "It's the books."

It feels like we've been running forever, our pounding steps sending up fresh clouds of dust. When we first walked down this corridor, books were lined neatly on the shelves, stretching as far as the eye could see. But now, as we run, I can see them scattered everywhere. It looks like the place has been ransacked, the books torn from the shelves and strewn across the floor. Everything is covered in a layer of dust that's getting thicker by the second.

I peer ahead into the gathering gloom and see the gap between the towering stacks begin to widen. We must be nearing the place where we started. I can hear voices in the distance getting louder as we run. I only hope the others have had better luck than we have.

"Ami!"

I hear Ibrahim's shout as we burst into the open and I turn to see him standing in the shadow of the information point. Oscar's there too, staring at the screen; the spindly arms that branch off its trunk offer no shelter from the dust that's falling all around.

"Did you find it?" Ibrahim asks as Adjoa and I try to catch our breath.

He's holding a book, and I recognize it right away.

A Natural Treasury

It's the same book that I found at Collection Point A.

Adjoa pulls our copy from her pocket. "We found it," she says, flicking through the book to show Ibrahim its empty pages. "But it doesn't tell us anything."

"Mine's the same," Ibrahim says. "When I first opened it, I thought I saw something written inside, but the words just seemed to turn into dust."

I remember pulling the book from the shadows of the shelf. There were words written in Adjoa's too, their jagged lines seared into my memory.

The sound of Oscar slamming his fist against the screen shatters my concentration. Turning around, he brandishes the same book.

"It's useless," he shouts. "I've tried scanning this book a million times, but the stupid machine keeps telling me the same thing."

Peering over his shoulder, I read the message that's displayed on the screen.

RESERVATION NOT RECOGNIZED
PLEASE TRY AGAIN

"These books are a waste of time," he growls. "I knew Min was talking nonsense when she said we'd find the Answer here."

"Where is Min?" I ask, suddenly realizing that we're not all here.

"I don't know," Ibrahim says. "We split up, remember?"

The library seems to growl in reply, a low, rumbling sound that shakes the air. I glance at the seething cloud above our heads, a swirling mass of dust that's getting darker by the second. As the falling specks land on my lips, a strange sensation shudders through me and I quickly wipe the dust away.

"This is bad," Adjoa shouts, raising her voice above the clamor. "This is really bad."

I look around, seeing the dark hexagonal desk still unattended in the center of the library. There's no librarian standing there ready to shush us. I don't know what we're supposed to do now. All I can think is that we've got to get out.

I crane my neck, trying to peer down the labyrinth of shelves. And then I see Min stumble clear of the stacks.

10

Min staggers toward us, her face gray with dust.

I just manage to reach her before she falls to the floor and I feel her dead weight sag in my arms.

"Is she okay?" Ibrahim asks, racing to my side to help me drag Min into a sitting position against the library desk.

"I don't know," I say as I watch her eyelids flutter.

Oscar appears at my shoulder. "Did she find anything?" he says. "Did she find the book?"

Adjoa starts to shush him, but then Min opens her eyes wide.

"I found the book," she replies, the words escaping from her lips in a giggle. "I found so many books. Big books, little books, true books and lies. And I ate them all up."

Min giggles again and then sticks her tongue out at us. I see with a shudder that it's stained black with dust.

A fresh peal of thunder crashes through the library, the sound rolling down the stacks. I rest my hand on Min's shoulder, leaning close to find out what's gone wrong. "What happened, Min?"

Her eyes blink again and then open wide as if seeing me for the first time.

"It hurts," she says, her voice trembling as she reaches up to touch the side of her head. "In here. It's like the dust is talking to me."

She looks like a gray ghost as she stares at me with haunted eyes. "I thought I'd find the Answer, but all I can see is darkness." Then Min starts coughing and I think she's never going to stop.

It's getting darker by the second; the blackened air is so thick that I'm finding it hard to breathe.

"What about the books?" Adjoa calls, her voice almost lost in the deluge of dust. "There must be something we can do."

Shielding my eyes, I stare into the darkness, feeling hopeless. All the books in the world can't save us now. It's their words that are choking us.

But as I look up into this sky of dust, some words are shaken loose inside my head.

There is another sky . . .

Dust rolls like thunder down the stacks, but I grab hold of these words. This means something.

"We need to use our minds," I shout, turning to face the others. In their hands, Adjoa, Oscar, and Ibrahim still hold *A Natural Treasury,* and I reach out to snatch the slim volume from Adjoa's grasp. "I thought I saw a poem in this book, but

it must have been a puzzle. If we can solve it, then we'll find
the way out."

"What did it say?" Ibrahim asks, his voice muffled as he
covers his mouth with his sleeve. "The words in my book disappeared before I could even read them."

I flip through the book, and it falls open at the same place
as before. The page is blank, but I can still see the words inside
my head as I recite them out loud.

"There is another sky,
Ever serene and fair,
And there is another sunshine,
Though it be darkness there;
Never mind faded forests,
Never mind silent fields—
Here is a little forest,
Whose leaf is ever green. . . ."

I look up from the page to see darkness everywhere.
Shadows spill from the heights of the towering stacks, books
floating like flotsam in this relentless avalanche of dust. The
swirling air is thick with choking specks, the sharp taste sting-
ing my throat. We're trapped in a library of dust and I don't
know what this puzzle means.

I hear Ibrahim muttering, the sound all but lost in the
tumult.

"Here is a little forest, whose leaf is ever green. . . ."

His eyes seem to gleam as he reaches the end of the line. Turning toward me, he raises his hands to the sky.

"This is the forest," Ibrahim shouts, gesturing around at the labyrinth of shelves. "Think about it. What is a library but a forest of books?" He holds up his own book, its pages flickering as the dust rains down. "And inside every book are the leaves."

I stare at Ibrahim, astounded. He's found the key to unlock the puzzle, but I still don't know what we have to do.

Half blinded by the dust, I look around in desperation. Through the choking haze my gaze falls on the information point, its strange metal structure rocked by the oncoming storm. As I stare, each jagged breath rasping in my lungs, I suddenly realize that it reminds me of something else. The broad trunk with its spindly arms branching in every direction. The shape of a tree.

And that's what we need to breathe.

I look down at the book in my hands. "Every book was a tree once," I shout, raising my voice above the thunder of dust. "And that's what we need now. We're choking to death, and trees make the oxygen we breathe. We need to build a tree."

"That's the stupidest thing I've ever heard," Oscar sneers, his face set in a snarl as the darkness falls. "How are we supposed to build a tree?"

Min coughs again, and I see that she's holding something

out to me. It's a page she's torn from her book, but she's folded it into a new shape. It looks like a leaf, its crisp edges pinched to a point while its pleated stem twists between her fingertips.

"There's an old Chinese proverb," Min says, still struggling to catch her breath. "The best time to plant a tree was twenty years ago. The second-best time is now."

I take the origami leaf from her, suddenly realizing what we have to do.

"The tree is already here," I say, pointing toward the bare branches of the information point, nearly lost in the storm. "All it needs are the leaves."

As the dust swirls, I sprint toward the structure, the origami leaf trembling in my hand. I can taste grit between my teeth, a fresh gale of words raging in my head. I try to put these out of my mind, focusing on the one thing that I need to do now.

Reaching the machine, I brush a thick layer of dust from the screen and stare at the message there as the darkness rains down.

RESERVATION NOT RECOGNIZED
PLEASE TRY AGAIN

With trembling fingers I place the origami leaf in the empty space beneath the display and watch as the thin red line of the laser slithers across the folded paper. I hear a whirring noise and glance up to see one of the metallic arms start to turn as a new message appears on the screen.

RESERVATION ACCEPTED
PLEASE PLACE IN THE SLOT

It's worked. Reaching up, I grab hold of the revolving arm, scrabbling to find the thing that it's told me to search for. Then I feel it, a tiny slot notched on the cylindrical branch. Fumbling, I slide the stem of the leaf into the slot and step back to see what happens next.

A faint gleam of sunlight seems to shine on the folded paper, a golden brightness that shimmers in the dark. The words of the puzzle poem chime inside my head: *There is another sunshine. . . .* Then the origami leaf starts to unfold itself, the paper rustling as it slowly turns green, as if it's remembering what it used to be—the origami shape transformed Pinocchio-like into the leaf of a real tree.

I stare, astonished, the lone leaf shining green as dust swirls. Then a new message appears on the screen.

NEXT RESERVATION PLEASE

Spinning on my heels, I turn to face the others. Min is still slumped in the shadow of the desk.

"It works!" I shout as fresh thunder rolls through the library. "We need more leaves!"

Racing back to Min, I rip a page from my book and hold it out to her. Still coughing, Adjoa, Oscar, Ibrahim, and I watch as she folds it in half, doubles over the corners and the edges, and then tucks in the little flaps, every crease making it look more like a leaf.

Her face is ashen as she holds it up for me to take. "Quickly, Ami."

I race back to the information point as the others start to tear their own books apart. Scanning the paper, I get the same message again, another arm of the machine swinging around for me to slot the leaf into place. Adjoa and Ibrahim are following Min's lead, folding the torn pages from their books into origami leaves. Even Oscar seems to be joining in, a mad grin on his face as he rips the pages out.

We race back and forth to the information point, every leaf scanned and slotted into the tree. It looks more real with every passing second, the branches glistening green as they reach toward a sky still seething with dust.

Then I hear another crack of thunder, much louder than the previous ones. And I watch as the dark trunk of the information point starts to open up.

"This way," Oscar shouts, scrambling toward the widening crack. "There's a way out."

As the dust swirls, I watch him squeeze through the gap, Ibrahim and Adjoa close behind him. I follow too, but then I glance back to see Min still slumped in the shadow of the library desk.

She won't make it on her own.

I race back to Min's side, trying not to breathe in the dust as a hard rain hammers down on us both. Her eyes are closed, and I have to lean close to check that she's still breathing.

"Wake up, Min," I say, shaking her shoulder. "We've got to get out."

Min's eyelids flutter open. "I had a dream," she says, her glazed eyes staring at me. "I dreamed I was a butterfly."

For a second a faint smile plays across Min's lips. Then a coughing fit overcomes her. She covers her mouth with her sleeve, bending forward as rasping barks rack her slender frame. Each hacking cough sounds as if it might be her last, and when she pulls her hand away, I see black specks on her sleeve.

With frightened eyes she stares up at me as the dust storm rages. "Now I feel like I'm a butterfly dreaming it's a girl."

"It's okay," I say. "I'm going to get you out of here."

I reach for Min's hand, but instead she grabs hold of my arm. Her fingernails dig into my skin as another coughing fit starts.

"Don't you understand, Ami?" she says as the coughs finally subside, her words coming in shuddering gasps. "I was wrong. I wasn't dreaming before. This is the dream. I am the butterfly."

I stare at Min. What she's saying makes no sense. I think the dust has poisoned her mind.

"Ami!"

A shout makes me turn my head. Through a blinding cloud of dust I glimpse Adjoa, her face framed by the darkened gate now cut into the base of the information point.

"You've got to get out now," she yells. "It's starting to close."

"Come on," I say, struggling to pull Min upright as I sling her arm around my shoulder. "I'm not leaving you."

Through the storm I stumble toward the information point, Min a dead weight by my side. The swirling dust cuts into us like tiny daggers; each snatched breath I take scrapes at my throat. I feel myself retch, coughing out a blackened spray of phlegm as I reach the shelter of the leaves. I glimpse the dark hollow cut into the metal trunk and scramble toward it, praying there's still time to get out.

The gate is closing with a grinding noise, the vibrations shaking this strange metal tree. I go first, as the gap's too narrow for us to fit through together, and Adjoa reaches out to pull me through. I turn to do the same for Min, but she takes a step away.

"Come on," I shout, feeling the sharp metal start to press against my shoulders. "I can't keep it open much longer."

Min shakes her head, her face framed by a halo of dust. "I need to wake up," she says, taking another step backward. "Goodbye, Ami. Please find the Answer for me."

I reach out, gritting my teeth against the pain as the closing gate groans. But when my fingers brush Min's, I feel her disintegrating.

"No!" I shout as Min turns to dust. One moment she's there, and the next she's gone as the darkness swarms around her.

I stare out in horror at the seething storm, unable to believe what I've just seen.

Then I feel myself dragged backward, and the gate closes with a clang as the ground crumbles beneath my feet.

11

Rocks tumble around me as I fall. It's like I'm caught in a landslide, pitched forward and downward into the dark. I feel my body twist, my legs desperately bicycling against empty air. I keep trying to grab hold of something in the blackness, but nothing meets my hands. . . .

BAM!

My shoulder crashes against stone, the impact knocking the breath out of me. It's like I've been slammed into a brick wall, and I sprawl on the ground in pain.

For a moment I don't move, trying to work out if I've broken anything. All I can hear in the darkness are my own juddering breaths. Then I see a flicker of light, which brightens with a crackle to form a spreading orange glow.

Every part of me aches as I pull myself upright. The others are scrambling to their feet too. We seem to be standing in some kind of chamber, the light coming from a burning torch that's fixed high on the nearest wall. The stone walls are covered in carvings, the strange figures of monsters and men looming in the gloom. Unlike the endless library of dust that we've just escaped from, this chamber is only about ten meters long and maybe half as wide. In the center of the room is what looks like a solid-stone table, the rough floor around it strewn with bones. They look human. . . .

Over my shoulder, I see a vaulted stairway choked with rubble. This must be the landslide that brought us here: a wall of stone that shows no way out.

I turn back to face the others; the three of them are staring straight at me.

Adjoa's the first to speak.

"Where's Min?"

Her dark braids frame an expression of real worry, her lips pursed as she waits for my reply. But as I meet Adjoa's gaze, all I can see in my mind is Min's face turning to dust.

"She's gone," I say, struggling to speak. "I tried to pull her back, but she didn't want to come. The door was closing, the dust swarming everywhere. I watched her disintegrate. . . ."

My words trail away as I feel a tear rolling down my face.

There's a moment of silence and then Oscar laughs out loud. "Yeah, right," he says. "You're such a sucker, Ami."

"What do you mean?" I say, staring at him in disbelief. "Didn't you hear what I said? Didn't you see what was happening out there?"

Oscar sniffs, wiping the dust from his face with the back of his sleeve. "Special effects," he replies. "That's all it was. The fire, the dust, the disappearing Min—it's all just part of the story. This is the ultimate escape game, remember?"

"This isn't a game," I say, raising my voice to a shout. My gaze falls on the scattered bones and I feel my heart twist. "I just watched Min crumble into dust."

"That's what they want you to *think* you saw," Oscar says, brushing dust from his hands. "Min wasn't one of us. She knew too much—just think about all those hints she gave. She was part of the game, and now they've gotten her out of the way to see how we cope on our own."

Standing close by, Ibrahim slowly nods.

"I've heard that some escape rooms do this," he says. "Put a person on the team playing the game to keep tabs on them. They'll give clues if they see the team getting stuck, but they never let on that they're really an actor."

"You see," Oscar says, nodding in Ibrahim's direction. "He knows what I'm talking about. Don't worry about Min—she'll be safely back with the Host. They're probably watching us right now." He looks around the chamber as if searching for a hidden camera. "So we need to show them we can find the Answer on our own."

"I know what I saw," I protest as Oscar turns away. I glance across to Adjoa, looking for support, but my friend just shrugs.

"Maybe he's right, Ami," she says.

It's like they're desperate to convince themselves that this is still a game.

A flicker of doubt creeps into my mind. How can I be sure

that what I saw was true? Surely Dad wouldn't have brought me here if he thought there was any chance of me getting hurt. I remember Min's fingers brushing against mine as I felt her start to disintegrate, but the clouds of dust could've hidden what was really happening. Maybe it *was* just smoke and mirrors. . . .

"So what is this place?" Oscar's gruff question pulls me back to the present. "Some kind of ancient ruin?"

I look around the vaulted chamber, its rough stone roof not much higher than our heads. Shadows dance across the sculpted walls, skulls and hieroglyphs hemming us in on every side. At least I know why they call this The Escape—there's no way out.

"We're inside a Mayan temple," Adjoa says, leaning closer to inspect the stone carvings. "This is the burial chamber."

"Who's Amaya?" Oscar sneers. "And why's she buried here?"

"The *Mayans* were an ancient civilization," Adjoa replies, ignoring the tone of Oscar's question. "They ruled for more than a thousand years, building great cities in the forests of Mexico and Central America. And then they just disappeared, abandoning their cities as their civilization collapsed. Their palaces and pyramids lay hidden for centuries, lost deep in the jungle, until their ruins were discovered by intrepid explorers."

"Wait a minute," Ibrahim says, raising his hand as if asking a question in class. "I thought it was the ancient Egyptians who built the pyramids."

Adjoa shakes her head. "The Mayans built pyramids too,

with steep steps on every side. At the top was a temple where priests carried out human sacrifices, while inside the pyramids, explorers found secret tunnels, chambers, and traps. That's where we must be now: inside the heart of a Mayan pyramid."

"How do you know all this?" I ask, not sure where Adjoa is pulling all these facts from. "Were you reading *The Rough Guide to Ancient Civilizations* while I was climbing that ladder back in the library?"

Adjoa grins in reply. "The thirteenth level of *Tomb Raider: Underworld* is set in a Mayan temple," she says. "That's how I recognized these hieroglyphs. I told you this game was made for me."

Ibrahim frowns as he looks around the chamber. "So we just need to find the secret tunnel and avoid the traps, right?"

"We need to find the Answer," Oscar says, striding toward the long stone table in the middle of the floor. "So get looking."

Sticking out her tongue behind Oscar's back, Adjoa still follows his order, turning away from the Mayan hieroglyphs to start searching the chamber. Pushing all thoughts of Min out of my mind, I follow her lead, looking around for any kind of clue. I think the only way out of this game is to win it.

Glancing at the desiccated bones strewn around my feet, I recognize ribs, femurs, and vertebrae from the pages of my encyclopedia. They're definitely human. A shudder runs down my spine as I stare into the eye sockets of a cracked skull as its yellowed teeth grin back at me.

"Are these the bones of the people who were buried here?" I ask, my voice echoing off the walls even though it's barely more than a whisper.

Adjoa shakes her head. "They're human sacrifices," she says, stepping over the jumbled cascade of bones. "When a Mayan noble died, their servants were killed to accompany them into the afterlife." She points to the long stone table Oscar is standing behind. "That's who's buried here."

Stepping closer, I realize that it isn't a table but a sarcophagus. A solid slab of stone rests on top of the monolithic coffin, swirling patterns and hieroglyphs carved into its flagstone lid. Near the top, I see a small circular hollow and catch a glint of red deep inside this spyhole. It reminds me of the red dot I saw in the center of the camera lens and the one that gleamed from the black pearl in the chess player's turban. In my mind I hear the whisper of the Host's words again. *I will be monitoring your every move.*

Oscar was right. He's watching us now.

Leaning closer, Adjoa is already inspecting the strange carvings. The largest is a circle with swirling spirals set inside.

"This is the symbol of Hunab Ku," she says, her voice hushed as her fingers trace the outline of the circle. "Some say the Mayans believed he was the god who created everything."

"He should know what the Answer is, then," grunts Oscar.

I'm expecting Adjoa to roll her eyes at Oscar's interruption, but instead she nods eagerly.

"He should," she replies, her dark eyes gleaming with excitement. "Don't you see, this means we're on the right track. The Mayans believed that Hunab Ku lived in the center of the Milky Way—that's what this spiral shape represents, the galaxy we live in. Others call it the Galactic Butterfly. Some say the symbol of the Hunab Ku shows the gateway to all knowledge, so this must be where the Answer is."

Oscar cracks his knuckles with a grin. "Then let's get the lid off this thing."

12

"It's useless," Oscar shouts, stepping away as he wipes the sweat from his face. "You bunch of weaklings are no help at all."

We've been trying to shift this solid slab of stone for what feels like hours, the four of us straining to push the lid off the sarcophagus to reveal the contents. But in all that time we haven't managed to move it even a centimeter. It weighs a ton.

"Says you," Adjoa snaps in reply. "Here's the one puzzle that needs brute force instead of brains, and it turns out you're all mouth."

As the two of them start to argue, I turn away with a heavy sigh. Adjoa seems convinced that the Answer lies inside this sarcophagus, but I can't shake the feeling that something's not quite right. I look around the gloom of the burial chamber, peering into the flickering shadows as I try to work out what's wrong.

Ibrahim is crouching close to the floor, his head bent as he peers at something that he's found there.

"What is it?" I ask, wondering if he's feeling the same as me.

Brushing his dark hair away from his face, Ibrahim glances up at me with a pensive frown. "I've found these bones."

I look down at the skeletal bones scattered in the dust.

"I know," I say, feeling a prickle of fear creep across my skin. "Horrible, isn't it? Adjoa says they were sacrificed."

Ibrahim nods. "And it looks like they did something to them too." He picks up one of the bones and shows it to me. "See?"

The bone he's holding looks like a femur—the long bone you find in the upper leg. This one is about half a meter long, but as Ibrahim turns it over I see that there's something strange about it. One end is rounded, like normal, but the other end seems to have been sharpened to a chisel edge.

"Is it a weapon, do you think?"

Taking the sharpened bone from his hand, I try to work out what it might have been used for. I don't think it's a weapon—it's not a spear or a sword, even though its edge looks sharp enough to cut. Strangely, the shape of it reminds me more of a doorstop. Although here, there's no door to hold open. . . .

I look up to meet Ibrahim's gaze. His head is tilted slightly, as if he's trying to look at the world from a different angle. I remember what Adjoa called him as we walked through the stacks in the library. She said he was a *finder*—someone who sees the things everyone else has missed. This bone must be important somehow.

I hear a hand slapping against stone and look back to see Oscar and Adjoa still arguing across the sarcophagus lid.

"If we can't lift it, then we'll just have to break it open," Oscar growls.

Adjoa was right: Oscar's a destroyer.

But as I look from the flagstone lid of the sarcophagus to the chiseled bone I'm holding, an idea slides into the front of my mind. Maybe this puzzle needs brains rather than brute force after all. . . .

Clambering to my feet, I head back to Oscar and Adjoa. As the two of them bicker, I peer at the edge of the sarcophagus, where the heavy lid meets the stone coffin beneath. It's almost a perfect seal, but in a couple of places I see cracks and slivers where the stone has been chipped away. They're only knife-thin, but if my idea is going to work, I hope this will do the trick.

Carefully lining up the bone, I place its chiseled edge against one of the cracks.

"What are you doing?" Oscar asks, casting a dismissive glance in my direction.

"Lifting the lid," I reply.

"On your own? With a bone?" Oscar laughs. "You've got no chance."

"It's not a bone, it's a lever," I tell him, sliding the edge between the base and the lid of the sarcophagus. "And with the right lever you can move the whole world."

With all the strength I can muster I pull down hard on the rounded end of the bone.

The lid lifts, only millimeters at first, but as I strain to force the lever down, the gap widens, and the flagstone lid rumbles away before crashing to the floor with a deafening boom.

Oscar jumps back with a yelp of surprise.

Breathing hard, I stand stock-still for a second, still holding the sharpened bone. It actually worked. But there's no time to catch my breath as the others quickly crowd around the now-open sarcophagus.

"You did it," Adjoa says, reaching out to squeeze my hand as I join her there. "That was incredible, Ami! Now we can find out what the Answer is."

Oscar lets out a low whistle as he peers inside the sarcophagus. "Who cares what the Answer is," he says. "It looks like we've found ourselves some treasure here."

A skeleton lies on its back inside the sarcophagus, its bones perfectly preserved. Surrounding it are countless pieces of exquisite jewelry: jade necklaces, silver bracelets, and golden rings. Beads of malachite and pearl lie scattered among tiny carved figurines, but it's not the sight of this treasure that makes me gasp. It's the layer of bright-red dust that covers it all.

"I'll take this," Oscar says, reaching for a crown that rests on top of the crimson skull. But before he can grab it, Adjoa knocks his hand away.

"Don't touch it!" she shouts, her voice thick with fear. "That red dust is cinnabar."

"So what?" Oscar says, turning angrily toward her. "This stuff's worth a fortune—a bit of cinnamon isn't going to do me any harm."

"Not cinnamon," Adjoa replies, standing her ground as Oscar tries to stare her down. "*Cinnabar*. It means 'dragon's blood,' and it's the most toxic mineral on earth. Just one touch can kill you." The flickering light cast by the torch makes her eyes shine. "It's the perfect booby trap."

Oscar takes a step back from the dust-encrusted crown, but Ibrahim is still peering inside the sarcophagus.

"Who do you think this is?" he asks.

Adjoa looks down at the crimson skeleton. "It's the Red Queen of Palenque," she says, keeping her voice low, as if she's afraid of waking the dead. "A Mayan noblewoman whose tomb was found in the thirteenth temple of a lost city, deep in the jungles of Mexico. Nobody knows her true identity, but the treasures she was buried with led some to believe she was the last Mayan queen. Her body was painted with this dust because it was the same color as the rising sun and the Mayans thought it would give her the power to rise as well. The Red Queen would live again."

I shiver at the thought, then glance back over my shoulder at the rest of the bones, scattered among our footprints in the dust. No chance of a new life for any of those people. Maybe the ones with the treasure are the only ones that matter. . . .

"I thought you said we'd find the Answer in here," Oscar growls, still looking annoyed that he can't get his hands on these riches. "What was the point of opening the lid if it doesn't take us anywhere? There's no gateway here, just a pile of dusty old bones."

Adjoa frowns, but this time she has no reply. I look again at the crimson skeleton, every piece of treasure caked in the poisonous dust. Maybe Oscar's right. Maybe this is just a red herring. . . .

But as my gaze roams across the riches draped over the Red Queen's bones, I glimpse something that seems out of place. Fine pieces of jewelry shine beneath the dust, but between her skeletal fingers the Red Queen seems to be holding a simple seashell.

In my mind I hear the Host's words: *The Answer might be found in the most unexpected of places.*

I pull a handkerchief from my pocket and use it to cover my hand, then reach inside the sarcophagus.

"Careful, Ami," Adjoa breathes as I ease the seashell from the Red Queen's grasp. "Don't touch the dust."

The outside of the seashell is painted copper-red, and as I turn it over carefully in my hand, I see a carving hidden inside. It's shaped like a butterfly, its wings marked with the same pattern as the sarcophagus lid. There's no dust inside the shell, so I carefully pick the carved object out with my free hand before dropping both the shell and the handkerchief back into the open coffin.

As I stare down at the stone butterfly, the others crowd around for a closer look.

"What is it?" Oscar asks.

"I'm not sure," I reply, holding the tiny sculpture to the light.

As the torchlight flickers, stripes of gold shimmer across the butterfly's wings. I know it's only a trick of the light, but the butterfly looks like it's about to take flight.

"It's the Galactic Butterfly," Adjoa says, the ghost of a smile creeping across her lips. "The Hunab Ku."

As she says this, excitement sparks in my chest. Adjoa said before that the Hunab Ku shows the gateway to all knowledge. I glance at the stone walls that surround us, at the gods and monsters guarding this place. This butterfly seems to be carved from the same stone, almost like it should fit somewhere here. And as I stare at the strange hieroglyphs that mark the end wall of the chamber, something seems to click inside my mind.

"If we're looking for the Answer, maybe this is the key."

Still holding the stone butterfly, I walk toward the far wall, searching for what I know must be there.

"What are you looking for?" Ibrahim asks, hurrying to join me.

My fingers trace the hieroglyphs, the patterns they make swirling across the solid stone. The graven faces of jaguars and alligators stare sightlessly back at me, their teeth bared in snarls, as if I'm trespassing.

"A way out," I tell him, still searching for a place where the carving might fit. "That's what we've been looking for all along. The hatch in the attic, the door in the library—this game is called The Escape, so that's what must be hidden here: some kind of gate that will let us escape." I glance down at the stone butterfly. "And I think this is the key we need to open it."

I look back at the wall, peering into its shadowy cracks and crevices. As well as the strange faces of beasts and men, I can see seashells, circles, and lines sculpted in the stone.

"What do you think they mean?" Ibrahim asks, his gaze following mine as we trace the spirals of the hieroglyphs. But before I can answer, Adjoa jumps in with her reply.

"I think they tell the time," she says, suddenly appearing right by my side.

Behind us, I hear a sniggering laugh.

"You mean like a clock?" Oscar says, swaggering up to us as we scour the wall for clues. "Well, it looks like it's stopped."

I know he's trying to be funny, but as I stare at the circular patterns that the hieroglyphs make, I can't help but think that it *does* look like a giant clock face.

"It's not a clock," Adjoa replies, reaching toward the outermost circle, where midnight would strike. "It's a calendar." She starts to trace the shape, passing over each of the carved hieroglyphs as they spiral around. "The Mayans had not just one calendar, like people do today, but three. This is the Haab, a solar calendar that lasts for three hundred sixty-five days. Each of these symbols is a Mayan month—Zotz, Tzec, Xul, Yaxkin, and more—eighteen months that each lasted for twenty days." As her hand sweeps to the start of the circle again, Adjoa pauses, her fingers hovering over a strange hieroglyph that looks like a screaming mouth. "And a nineteenth month of five nameless days that the Mayans called the Wayeb. This was a time of great danger, when the Mayans believed the gates to the underworld were opened and chaos was unleashed on the world."

Adjoa's hushed words echo off the walls of the tomb and I feel my skin prickle with fear. We might be looking for a gate, but as I stare at these carved jaws, I just hope it isn't the one to the underworld.

Adjoa starts to trace a second circle of hieroglyphs, a wheel within a wheel.

"This is the Tzolkin," she says. "It's the calendar the Mayans used to mark their sacred days. Feasts, festivals, and ceremonies—all were determined by the Tzolkin. The Mayans believed it could even predict the future."

Mesmerized, I watch as Adjoa's fingers follow the hieroglyphs, shadows falling across the eerie carvings.

"The Mayans saw time not as a straight line," she explains, "but as a circle. History repeats itself—what has happened before will happen again. The Mayans believed that time was an endlessly turning cycle that went on and on."

"Just like you," Oscar mutters under his breath.

Adjoa ignores him, her fingers coming to rest in the center of the circle.

"Until the end of the Long Count," she says. "This is the calendar the Mayans used to count the days since the world was created. An age they believed would last for two million, eight hundred and eighty thousand days."

Adjoa moves her hand away from the wall and I see the cluster of hieroglyphs that mark the Long Count. The sculpted shapes of monstrous faces leer back at me, skull-like birds and jaguars. Nestled in the center of them I see the shadow of a hollow in the stone. Peering closer, I see that this tiny cavity has been carved in the shape of a butterfly, and as I compare it to the stone I'm holding, I realize it's a perfect match.

"This is it," I say, noticing a faint red glow that seems to emanate from deep inside the hollow. "I think we've found the keyhole."

13

I hold the stone butterfly between my fingertips, the spiral patterns on its wings lit with an eerie red glow. It looks as though it's been carved from this hollow, the red light gleaming deep inside. It's the same light I've seen all the way through this game—the one that's telling me now that I must be right.

As the others crowd around my shoulders, I carefully place the butterfly inside the keyhole, feeling the carving click into place.

"It fits," Adjoa whispers, her voice hushed in the shadows.

Holding my breath, I wait to see what happens next, but as the seconds stretch into silence, I'm forced to let it out again in a puzzled sigh.

"This can't be right," I say, peering closer to see a faint glow still glimmering around the edge of the butterfly's wings. "It hasn't worked."

"It *has* to work," Adjoa says. "It all fits—the gateway, the butterfly, the Hunab Ku. This has to be the key."

I turn around, looking to the others for any kind of clue. Ibrahim frowns, his fingers fidgeting as if the hieroglyphs are a scrambled Rubik's cube for him to solve. Oscar has his arms folded nonchalantly across his chest and a know-it-all look on his face.

"What is it?" I snap, his smirk already annoying me.

"If you think it's a key," Oscar says slowly, as if I'm stupid, "don't you need to turn it?"

I blink. He's right.

Facing the wall again, I reach for the butterfly. The carved stone feels smooth, but as I start to turn it, I hear a juddering sound like the grinding of ancient gears. The spiraling hieroglyphs suddenly shine with an eerie red light, and I watch as the wheels start to turn.

"It's working," Adjoa says, a buzz of excitement in her voice. "Keep turning."

As I slowly twist the stone butterfly, the hieroglyphs continue to revolve. Mesmerized, I watch as the snarling stone faces wheel around, the roar of hidden machinery making the wall shake. As it turns, the outer wheel seems to be counting the months off, the symbols that Adjoa showed us glowing red as each one glides by, while the inner wheel seems to turn back time as it revolves counterclockwise. I keep on turning the key, waiting for a click that never comes.

"I don't understand," I say, raising my voice over the clattering noise. "If this is the gate, why won't it open? What else do we need to do?"

"Let me try," Oscar says, pushing me out of the way to get his hand on the key. "I have a knack for these things."

But as he turns the butterfly key, the concentric rings of hieroglyphs just keep spinning, the tomb shaking as they revolve in opposite directions. I glance up in fear as shards of stone start to fall from the ceiling. If we don't stop turning the wheels, we're going to be buried alive. The crimson glow seems to seep through the carved symbols and faces, the color blood-red, but there's no sign of any gate starting to open.

"Maybe it's not a gate," Ibrahim says, almost as if he's reading my mind. "Maybe this is more like the door to a safe that's keeping the Answer locked away. The only way to open it is to find the right combination."

I look across at Ibrahim, his head tilted to one side as he watches the hieroglyphs turn.

"This isn't just a calendar, it's a time lock," he says.

As his words sink in, the revolving symbols seem to sharpen. It's like my brain is tuning out all the noise and distractions to focus on the one thing that matters. It's not tunnel vision—it's puzzle vision. And if Ibrahim's right, the hieroglyphs are hiding the Answer. I turn toward Adjoa, her brow furrowed as she watches the wheels turn. "We need to find the right date to open the gate."

She nods in reply, her gaze fixed on the turning wheels as rocks tumble from the ceiling of the tomb.

"The Long Count lasts for two million, eight hundred and eighty thousand days. That's nearly eight thousand years. We can't try out every date in the hope of finding the right one by accident, but there's one date that made the Mayans famous. The twenty-first of December 2012—the day the Long Count said the world would come to an end." Her dark eyes shine in the flickering torchlight. "That's got to be the date that'll open the gate—the date that will give us the Answer and end this game once and for all."

I glance up at the stone carvings as the wheels in the wall continue to turn. The eerie red light that seems to seep through every hieroglyph glows brightest as they reach the highest point, before fading a little as they slip from the zenith. This must be the place where the date is marked, but as I stare at the spiraling stones I can't tell which of the symbols shows the end of the Long Count.

Adjoa, though, looks like she can. Elbowing Oscar out of the way, she grabs hold of the key and, gritting her teeth, starts to turn it more quickly. As the hieroglyphs whirl around with a clattering roar, Adjoa keeps her gaze fixed on the highest point of the wheel, watching as each carved face briefly blazes crimson before moving on to the next. Then she breathes a single word out loud: "Now."

With a squealing, grating roar the stone wheels judder to a halt as Adjoa stops turning the key. As rocks fall from the roof of the tomb, she points toward the hieroglyphs that shine the brightest.

"That's the end of the thirteenth *baktun*," she says, gesturing toward a sinister face halfway up the wall. "The last day of the Long Count. It has to be the right date."

As I stare at the stony profile, its single eye gleams red. Two more hieroglyphs are set directly above it, and I see with a shudder that the highest of these shows a skeletal jaw.

There's a second of silence, and then, directly behind me, I hear a scraping noise, like the sound of bone scratching against stone.

Turning around with a mounting sense of dread, I see the Red Queen slowly rising from her tomb.

14

"Get back!" Adjoa shouts, scrambling to escape as the crimson skeleton staggers toward us. "Don't let her touch you!"

Swathes of cinnabar dust fall from the Red Queen's fingers as she reaches out a skeletal claw. A jade crown hangs skewed atop her skull, her teeth bared in a ghostlike grin as a red light gleams from eyeless sockets. Frozen in fear, I can't pull myself away, my gaze locked on hers as the tomb shakes with a rumbling roar.

Oscar hammers on the wall, but the solid stone refuses to shift. "Let us out! Let us out!" he yells.

But the Host isn't listening. The Red Queen rules this place now.

Behind her, other skeletal figures are slowly picking themselves up from the floor, the bones of the Mayan dead rising again to serve their queen. I glance back at the wheels of hieroglyphs, trying to work out how we got everything so wrong.

At the highest point of the motionless wheels I see a

stone-carved scream. The skeletal jaws of the hieroglyph gape wide like an open gate. I remember the name Adjoa gave to this symbol—the Wayeb—the dangerous month of nameless days when the Mayans believed the gates to the underworld were opened. That's what we've done now—we've opened the gates to hell.

I hear a sudden hiss and I spin around to see the Red Queen standing right in front of me, her skeletal arms spread wide. As she lunges to wrap me in a deadly embrace, Adjoa drags me clear, the two of us stumbling backward as rocks plummet down. Slipping on loose stone, I feel my ankle twist and can't stop myself from falling to the floor.

Lifting my head, I see the Red Queen turning toward Ibrahim. He's standing in front of the spiraling hieroglyphs, his head bent as he inspects the stone butterfly that lies at its heart. He doesn't even seem to notice she's there, lost in thought as his fingers fidget and twitch in search of the Answer.

I open my mouth wide, ready to call out a warning, but then I catch sight of something crawling on the ground. It's not much bigger than a grain of rice, its spiky black body bristling as it wriggles forward in a wavelike motion.

It's a caterpillar.

The tiny creature is treading a perfect circle in the dust in front of my eyes. Its segmented body writhes as it winds its way around. The sight is strangely mesmerizing. Inside my head I hear the Host mocking me.

Look around carefully. Everything is part of the game.

This must *mean* something.

My mind races as I remember what Adjoa told me about the Mayans. How they thought time was an endlessly turning circle. I watch the caterpillar trace the same shape in the dust. I think about what I know about these tiny creatures, racking my brain for any kind of clue. How caterpillars live for only a couple of weeks. How they eat and eat and eat . . .

"Ibrahim!"

I hear Adjoa's anguished scream, but my gaze stays fixed on the circling caterpillar. Then I hear a whisper inside my head, Min's voice reminding me what comes next.

I dreamed I was a butterfly.

With a dawning realization I look up at the solid-stone wall. The wheels of hieroglyphs stand motionless, but as my eyes follow the spiraling shapes that they make, I realize the circle has no end. The end is the beginning. The caterpillar becomes a butterfly. . . .

My thoughts crystallize into cold, hard certainty. What I need to do now is suddenly very clear.

I scramble to my feet, heading straight for the center of the spiraling hieroglyphs. Close by, Adjoa looks on aghast as the Red Queen sways like a bone marionette, turning to face Oscar as he backs into a corner of the tomb.

"Come on!" he shouts, his eyes blazing with fury. "I'm not scared of you and your stupid army."

In reply to his shout I hear the scrape of bone against stone again as the Red Queen and her servants prepare to strike.

This is my chance—the split-second distraction I needed to grab hold of the butterfly key. The stone feels warm beneath my fingertips, the wings spread in perfect symmetry as I give the key one final twist.

There's a click and then the stone wheels start turning once more, trundling on to the next hieroglyph before stopping again with a shudder. The stone butterfly slips from my fingers, retracting into the hollow as I stagger back in surprise.

"Ami," Adjoa calls, her voice echoing off the shaking walls. "What have you done?"

I see a glint of gold at the heart of the hollow and watch as it starts to grow.

"I've changed the date," I reply as the golden gleam seems to flutter more brightly. There's something moving inside the widening hole. "It wasn't the last day of the Long Count that we needed, but the first day of the next. The circle keeps on turning. We can only find the Answer if we start again."

The hollow has now grown to the size of a small window, and it's getting bigger with every passing second. The hieroglyphs at the center of the stones start to crumble away, revealing the golden wings of countless butterflies. These start to stream through the opening gate, the butterflies pouring forth in a never-ending torrent.

The Red Queen screams as the butterflies swarm around her, her crimson bones disappearing beneath a beating tide of wings.

"This way!" I shout, calling to Adjoa and Oscar as the

tomb continues to shake. I can't see Ibrahim anywhere, just the bones of the Red Queen's servants flailing against the on-coming storm as the butterflies continue to swarm.

I hold my arm out in front of me, groping my way through this golden haze of fluttering butterflies. Oscar's already at the gate, clambering through as Adjoa appears by my side.

"Where's Ibrahim?" I shout, raising my voice above the rumbling thunder.

"It's too late, Ami," Adjoa moans, tears streaming down her face. "We've got to get out of this place."

She grabs hold of my arm and starts pulling me through the gate, the relentless tide of butterflies still streaming through. Beyond their golden wings, I glimpse blackness and the faint outline of metallic steps descending in the dark.

As Adjoa drags me with her and Oscar rushes ahead, all I can do is follow them down.

15

The metal stairs ring with our footsteps as we descend. I can see the outlines of Adjoa and Oscar ahead of me in the gloom, all of us walking now in single file as the handrails on either side guide us down in parallel lines.

I've stopped asking Adjoa what happened to Ibrahim in the tomb; her tearful replies only tell me that he's gone. Just like Min. This game is picking us off one by one.

There's a brightness spreading up ahead, and the stairs get shallower with every tread. I can see now that we're descending a ruined escalator, its frozen steps carpeted with shards of glass that crunch beneath my sneakers.

It looks like we're entering some kind of shopping mall. A huge clock hangs on the far side of a soaring atrium, the brightness coming from the skylights in its domed ceiling. Through these airy windows I can see a distant blue. The hands of the clock stand at twelve minutes past eight, but I can't really tell whether it's a.m. or p.m.

Oscar's the first to reach the final stair, his strides taking him across the empty concourse. I look around as I join Adjoa there and take in a scene of utter destruction. Piles of debris litter the wide-open space: shattered glass and ripped-out shelving, smashed display cabinets and broken plant pots. Near the center of the atrium, a drained fountain is filled with dust, while withered plants scatter trails of dead leaves across the tiles.

It looks like this place has been abandoned for years.

Oscar's still striding ahead, his echoing steps taking him past a deserted customer service desk.

"Where are you going?" I call out after him. "We've got to stick together, especially now."

Oscar stops in his tracks, turning toward me with a look of contempt.

"Why?" he replies, his shout causing a flock of wild pigeons to take flight from their hidden perches. As they soar toward the skylights, their slate-gray wings flecked with bronze, Oscar whirls on me. "Why do we have to stick together? It hasn't done us any good so far, has it? Take a look around, Ami. We're not the Five Mind or the Awesome Foursome. There's just the three of us now. We're not a team—we're competitors. And I'm going to make sure I find the Answer first."

Oscar turns to leave, tossing a final comment over his shoulder. "And don't even think about following me."

I stand there, dumbfounded, and watch him go. The path

he takes through the piles of broken things leads toward an arcade of shops. It's darker over there, away from the atrium's skylights, but I can just make out the sight of shuttered store-fronts.

"Let him go," Adjoa says, walking toward the customer service desk. "We don't need him."

I look around the deserted mall, more galleries of shops branching off to the left and right. These faded arcades are plunged into darkness too and, as I strain my eyes against the shadows, a shiver runs down my spine. This place should be filled with light and life. I'm not scared of the dark, but I can't stop myself from wondering what it's hiding. It's the fear of the unknown.

"Ami!" Adjoa's excited shout makes me turn. She's standing by the customer service desk, holding up a crumpled piece of paper. "Come and see what I've found."

Hurrying over, I take the scrap of paper from her, feeling puzzled as I read the words written there.

GOLDEN
FROZEN
JUMPER
HUNTER
EX I T

I look up at Adjoa and see a glint of delight sparkling in her eyes.

"What is it?" I ask, struggling to work out why she's so excited. The words don't make any sense at all.

"Isn't it obvious?" Adjoa replies with a grin. "It's a shopping list."

I look again at the list, turning each word over in my mind: *golden, frozen, jumper, hunter, exit.* I shake my head. If this is a shopping list, I don't know what it wants us to buy. Seeing my frown, Adjoa starts to explain.

"Remember what the Host said," she says, the toes of her neon-green sneakers tapping a fidgety rhythm on the floor. "Everything is part of the game. This list was left here, waiting for us. This must be a scavenger hunt."

"A scavenger hunt?"

"One of those games where you get a list of things to find. Some people call them treasure hunts, but the winner's always the one who's the first to get every item on the list. That must be what this is—a list of the things we need to find the Answer."

She takes the list back from me, turning again to face the customer service desk. The front edge slopes toward us, displaying a store directory and a map of the shopping mall. I can see the arcades branching off in three directions from this central atrium, the galleries of shops marked in red, green, and blue.

"This is our chance, Ami," Adjoa says as she inspects the color-coded map. "If we want to beat Oscar to the Answer, we just have to find the objects on this list."

I glance at the store directory. I didn't think our mission

to save the world would end with a shopping trip, but what Adjoa's saying kind of makes sense. Since we started playing The Escape, we've been trying to find the Answer, but nobody said it was just one thing. Maybe this list tells us the ingredients we need to *create* the Answer. And if she's right, this means we've got a head start on Oscar.

"So where do we go first?" I ask, trailing my finger down the list of shops, arranged by category. "Beauty and Fragrances? Books, Cards, and Stationery? Electronics? Entertainment? Fashion?"

Adjoa shakes her head, pointing instead to a heading halfway down the list.

"Jewelry," she replies with a confident smile. "The list says the first thing we're looking for is golden, so we're bound to find something there. A gold ring or a necklace, maybe—anything like that."

Her finger moves across to point out the store's location on the map, halfway along the left-hand gallery.

"After that we'll head to a grocery store to find something frozen," she continues, plotting out the route we'll take, "before moving on to fashion to grab ourselves a sweater—which British people call a jumper." Glancing up, Adjoa flashes me a grin. "We're going to finish this game in style."

I try to force a smile, but something's still troubling me.

"What about the other items?" I ask, reaching out to take the list from Adjoa again. "Where are we going to find a hunter?"

"We don't need to find a hunter," she replies. "We *are* the hunters, and once we get the objects on the list, we'll find the Answer too. It's all we need to finish the game and get out of this place. That's what 'EXIT' means—the end is in sight, Ami."

I meet my friend's gaze. Even though she's smiling, Adjoa's eyes look hollowed out, the tears she cried having left dark circles behind.

I think about Ibrahim and Min and all that we've seen so far. The burning attic and the library of dust, the cursed tomb, and now this deserted shopping mall. And as I think, I can't stop myself from asking the question out loud.

"Do you still think it's a game?"

Adjoa bites her lip, almost as if she's afraid to reply.

"It has to be," she says finally. "And we need to make sure we win."

Adjoa turns to head for the darkened arcade, following the route her finger drew. Glancing back over her shoulder, she beckons me. "Come on, Ami."

16

"What do you think happened here?" I ask, peering into the shifting shadows as we make our way along the darkened arcade. Broken glass crunches underfoot as we pass the shuttered storefronts, their facades dented and torn. We've got no flashlight to light our path, so we have to rely on the shafts of light that fall from cracked ceiling tiles, these faint patches of brightness illuminating the puddles and piles of debris that populate this place instead of people. "Where is everybody?"

"I don't know," Adjoa replies, close to me in the dark. "But at least we don't have to worry about standing in line for the sales."

I shiver as I spot a headless mannequin lying in the dust, the sight reminding me of the piles of bones in the Red Queen's tomb. SALE signs are strewn around the shop dummy, their labels proudly proclaiming that EVERYTHING MUST GO. But as I listen to the silence that fills the shopping mall, it looks like everything already has.

Everything's gone.

A wave of sadness crashes over me. Dad said the game was going to be the perfect gift, but all I've found inside The Escape is senseless destruction. This can't be what he meant for me. The only thing I've got left to cling to now is the hope that the Answer might make sense of everything. If we can find it . . .

"I think this is it," Adjoa says, interrupting my thoughts with a tug on my arm.

She's come to a halt in front of another faceless store, the name of the shop above the shutters peeled away, leaving only the last letters behind.

ELER

Just like all the other stores that we've passed, this jeweler's lies in darkness. Slatted metal shutters are pulled down in front, but it looks like someone has taken an axe to them. A huge jagged hole has been torn in the metal, its sharp edges curling outward as if highlighting the way in.

"Follow me," Adjoa says, taking the lead. She steps through shards of glass to squeeze through the gap in the shutters.

"Are you sure we should be doing this?" I ask as I follow her, a nervous feeling gnawing at my insides.

Adjoa doesn't answer right away; her sneakers crunch through broken glass as her silhouette is suddenly outlined with a strange blue light. "Look at this."

Somehow it's lighter inside the store, due to a luminescent glow that seems to rise from the ground. I look around, my brain struggling to make sense of what I see. It's like I'm looking at an underwater scene, the shattered glass that carpets the floor glinting with an iridescent light. It looks like a sea of shining things glimmering blue-green. At first I think the shapes are sparkling fish, but then I realize they're watches, their luminous faces and ticking hands glistening in the dark.

As my eyes adjust, I start to make out the smashed display cases, the glass cabinets shattered with their contents strewn across the floor. Amid the glowing watch dials, I can see the silvery trails of earrings and necklaces, sparkling like treasure on the ocean bed.

"I didn't think it would be this easy," Adjoa says, squatting close to the ground as she starts to search through the scattered jewelry. "There's got to be something golden here."

I'm about to start looking too when I hear a sound: soft padding footsteps that seem to be coming from the back of the store. I turn around, thinking it must be Oscar, on the trail of the Answer too, and then I see it.

Built like a bear, and just as tall, it prowls forward on four powerful legs. Its golden fur shines in the glimmering half-light as it pads toward me. I hold my breath, unable to believe what I'm seeing as I stare into the eyes of the biggest cat I've ever seen. These shine golden too, but it's the two long, sharp teeth curving down from its upper jaw that make my heart thump in fear.

It's a saber-toothed tiger.

"Now, this is pretty," Adjoa says, holding up a glittering necklace. "But I think it's platinum, not gold."

She hasn't seen it yet, her gaze still fixed on the trinkets scattered across the floor.

I want to shout—to warn Adjoa of what's happening—but the words die on my lips as I watch the tiger open its jaws wide. We came here looking for something golden, but I think it's found us instead.

And then the saber-toothed tiger pounces, springing forward with a guttural roar.

Time seems to slow to a crawl as I throw myself backward, my vision filled with teeth and claws. Their blades swipe the air where I was standing only moments before as the tiger lands with a snarl of frustration, its powerful claws grinding the shards of glass into dust.

"What the—"

Adjoa turns, her eyes opening wide in fear as she sees the extinct animal clawing the ground only meters away. Grabbing hold of her, I scramble for the exit, the saber-toothed tiger snarling at our heels. We squeeze through the gap ripped in the shutters, and the metal judders as the hulking creature slams its body against the slats.

I turn around, gripping the jagged metal edges as I try to push them closed to stop the creature from coming through. The shutters shake as the saber-tooth slams itself against them again; the metal groans as if the whole thing is going to come down.

"What is that?" Adjoa gasps, her voice frantic in my ear.

Gritting my teeth against the pain, I force the sharp edges together; the shutters shake again with a hideous scratching as the beast claws at the closing gap. It's impossible to know how long this barrier will hold it, but then, it's impossible to think it's even here. The saber-toothed tiger died out thousands of years ago.

We've got to get out of here. I turn around, staring into the shadows as I try to remember the way back. The darkened arcade looks different now, the hulking shapes of frozen statues looming in the gloom. The largest looks as big as an elephant, its shadowy bulk practically touching the ceiling as it blocks the path ahead.

Adjoa screams as the saber-tooth slams its body against the shutters again. The metal judders, dislodging tiles from the ceiling. As they fall, fresh shafts of light shine on the scene, illuminating the hulking shadow straight ahead.

What I thought was a statue is actually an animal, its colossal frame covered in a coat of thick reddish-brown hair. It stands on legs as thick as tree trunks, its broad sloping back rising to a peaked dome. I hear its coarse hair rustling as its massive head turns toward me, and then I see its long, curved tusks silhouetted like twin question marks in the half-light.

I blink—not just my eyes, but my brain too—unable to process what I can see right in front of me. And then the beast raises its trunk as it lets out a trumpeting call that shakes the entire mall.

It's a woolly mammoth.

17

I stand there, frozen, staring at a creature that shouldn't exist.

Its ivory trunks curve sharply toward me, maybe three meters long or more. Small woolly ears flank the sides of its strange domed head, and its dark eyes stare straight into mine. Then the metal shutters behind us rattle again violently with the snarling rage of the saber-tooth still caged inside.

The mammoth's trunk flies up into the air, blaring out another siren note of warning. I see shadows behind it in the darkness start to move, and I realize they're heading straight for us.

"Run!" Adjoa shouts, grabbing hold of my arm as the mammoth begins its charge. The ground shakes as we stumble toward the shelter of a candy stand. Ripped-out seats are piled up against the pastel-colored stall, and we cower behind them, crouching in fear as, over the sound of thunder, we hear a deafening chorus of trumpeting calls.

I watch openmouthed as the shadowy herd of woolly

mammoths crashes past our hiding place, their trunks lashing from side to side as they stampede. Lurching in panic, one of the frantic beasts slams against the darkened front of the jewelry store, its curling tusks tearing the shutters away.

As the mammoth reels, I hear the triumphant roar of the now-freed saber-toothed tiger. The sound of the stampede is slowly receding, but as the mammoth moves forward again with a shake of its head, I watch a golden shadow stalk its lumbering steps.

"What do we do now?" Adjoa whispers, her body pressed close to mine as we shelter behind our makeshift hiding place.

Raising my finger to my lips, I silently gesture for her to follow me as I start to creep in the opposite direction. In the distance I hear the mammoths trumpeting and hope that the saber-toothed tiger is following their trail, not ours.

The wide walkway that leads through the arcade of shops still lies in darkness, but as I step between the shadows, I think I can see more shapes in the dark. It's impossible to make out any details; faint shafts of light illuminate only silhouettes. But these pitch-black shadows are moving, the bulky shapes of animals emerging from obscurity. I can see bears and bison, giant deer with antlers so large they seem to span the entire gallery. I think I can see something that looks like a rhino but covered in a coat of thick, shaggy hair. And there are even stranger animals that I don't recognize, with sweeping horns and huge terrifying beaks.

I freeze. There's no way through this shadowy menagerie

and, as I hear the thundering tread of the mammoths be-hind us, no way back either. I glance around, looking for any way out.

Most of the stores lie in darkness, their shutters rolled down against the storm, but then I glimpse a faint crack of light from one of the shopfronts. Unlike the other shops, there are no shutters here. The front of this store is boarded up with plywood instead. In the semi-darkness I can just read the words RENOVATION WORK IN PROGRESS writ-ten across it.

The light is coming from a crack in the plywood showing the way in. Or maybe it's a way out.

"This way," I whisper, tugging at Adjoa's arm.

As quietly as we can, we hurry toward the boarded-up store. Peeling back one of the broken boards, I hold it open for Adjoa to clamber through and wince as the silvery light spills across the arcade. Glancing fearfully over my shoulder to check that none of the shadowy beasts have spotted us, I quickly follow her through, letting the heavy board swing back into place.

It's even brighter inside the store, and I blink as my eyes take a moment to adjust to the light. It's coming from a safety lamp that's positioned near the entrance, the full glare of its beam angled toward the store's interior. There I can see empty shelving units and clothes rails arranged in rows across a tiled floor. Half of these look like they're ready to be ripped out, the yellowing shelves cracked and broken, while others look brand new, standing shrink-wrapped in clear plastic film. Electric cables hang in places from the ceiling, their bare wires twined together like withered vines.

"What do we do now?" Adjoa says, keeping her voice low as we step farther into the store. "Those things out there . . ."

Her words trail off as we hear a skittering tread coming from the first aisle. Adjoa's hand grabs for mine, her fingernails digging into my skin. In my head, I see the golden cat, its teeth and claws coming straight for me.

The sound comes again; its hiccupping rhythm makes my heart leap. I wait for the creature to reveal itself as Adjoa moans in fear. Then the scampering stops and I see a tiny furry face peering around the end of the shelving unit.

I can't help but laugh as the creature hops around the corner, my worst fears dissolving in front of my eyes.

It's a baby kangaroo.

Shaking off Adjoa's hand, I crouch as the joey hops toward me. Its ash-brown pelt fades to gray as it reaches the end of its tail, while the fur on its belly is a soft sandy color. Standing upright, the baby kangaroo reaches only halfway to my knee, but as I stare into its eyes, shining like black pearls, I can't help feel that it's judging me.

"Hey," I say, keeping my voice gentle so as not to scare it.

The baby kangaroo chirps in reply. Then it hops up onto my lap and nestles in the crook of my arm.

"You shouldn't pick it up," Adjoa says, a note of warning in her voice. "It's a wild animal."

"Shhhhhh." I stroke the joey with my free hand, feeling the warmth of its soft, silky fur. "You'll scare it."

The kangaroo peers up at me inquisitively. There's a distinctive black mark on its face that reaches in a V from its nose to its eyes, while the lighter fur below is a buff-yellow color.

"Where have you come from?" I wonder out loud.

"I'm more worried about the rest of them," Adjoa replies, stealing a glance back toward the boarded-up storefront. "We still need to get out of here, Ami."

I nod and then frown as my hand snags on a strange square of material halfway down the joey's back.

"What's this?"

It looks like a label, and the kangaroo wriggles as I try to look more closely at it.

"Stay still," I tell it, trying to soothe the squirming animal as my fingers gently investigate the label, which seems to be stitched into its fur. The joey's ears prick up inquisitively as I start to read the writing on the label out loud.

"*The toolache wallaby, pronounced* too-late-shee, *was a native of Australia. The most elegant, graceful and swift member of the kangaroo family, the toolache wallaby was hunted to extinction by man. The last toolache lived for twelve years in captivity and died in 1939. . . .*"

My voice trails off as the wallaby looks up at me with bright eyes. I can't believe anyone would want to hurt something so beautiful. Nuzzling against my skin, the toolache makes a soft chirping sound as if it's trying to tell me something.

"It's okay," I say, still stroking its ash-brown fur. I can feel the warmth of its body next to mine. It feels so alive, but this label stitched into its fur makes it seem like a toy. "I'll keep you safe, Tooey."

The wallaby chirrups again, echoing the sound of its name. *Tchoo-ey.*

"That's right," I say. "I'm going to call you Tooey."

I smile at Adjoa, but my friend's brow is still furrowed in a frown.

"What's the matter?" I ask her. "Don't you think she looks like a Tooey?"

"It's not her name that's the matter, Ami," Adjoa replies, her face crinkling with worry lines. "It's the fact that she's even here."

"What do you mean?"

"Think about everything we've seen since we arrived inside this mall," Adjoa says, her anxious words worming their way inside my brain. "The saber-toothed tiger, the woolly mammoths, all those impossible creatures outside. Even this baby kangaroo—"

"It's a wallaby," I say, snuggling the creature close to me.

"It's not supposed to be here, Ami!" Adjoa snaps, the sharp sound of her voice making Tooey squirm in my lap. "None of these animals should be. They all died out years ago."

Still squatting, I shift uncomfortably as my brain ticks off the words from the list one by one.

GOLDEN
FROZEN
JUMPER

A sudden clatter makes me turn toward the boarded-up entrance, Tooey burrowing into my arms. Adjoa spins around, picking up a metal pole. Brandishing it like a weapon, she stands ready to defend us as we watch something push its way through the broken boards.

The safety lamp is aimed straight toward us; the glare of its beam makes it difficult to see. But as a shadowy shape staggers forward into the light, I realize—it's Oscar.

His black zip top looks like it's been shredded to pieces, and his joggers are torn at the knees. Breathing heavily, Oscar stares at us, wild-eyed.

"There are monsters out there," he babbles in a frantic rush. "I was attacked. I thought I was going to die."

Oscar sinks to his knees and I see for the first time the figure standing directly behind him.

"He saved me."

18

The short, stocky figure steps forward into the light.

He looks like a caveman. His bare chest and arms are covered with thick black hair, and a grimy fur that looks like an animal skin is wrapped around his waist. He glances toward Oscar as if checking that he's safe and then squats on his haunches.

"I don't believe it," Adjoa breathes, letting the pole she was holding slip from her fingers. "It's a Neanderthal."

I stare at the man. His broad-nosed face is framed by thick matted hair, and streaks of what looks like dried blood are daubed across his cheeks. And from beneath the jutting ridges of his bristling brows, the Neanderthal's dark eyes stare back at me.

I silently tick off the next word on the list: HUNTER.

"He brought me here," Oscar says, shuffling forward as Adjoa squats too, the four of us now hunkered in a loose circle. "I think he can help us."

Tooey wriggles in my lap as I shake my head in disbelief. I don't know what Oscar means. We came here looking for the Answer, not the Lost World. How can this caveman help us now? This isn't his time. This isn't his place.

"It's worth a try," Adjoa says, the sound of her voice in my ear surprising me. "Show him the list, Ami."

Buttoning up my jacket to keep Tooey safe inside, I pull the scrap of paper from my pocket and hold it out toward the caveman, my hand trembling slightly as I do.

"We're looking for the way out," I say, my thumb smudged against the final word. "The exit."

I stare into the Neanderthal's eyes, our minds separated by tens of thousands of years.

"Can you help us?"

The Neanderthal stares blankly at me. In the darkness of his eyes all I can see is my own reflection.

He doesn't know what I mean. He can't help us. Nobody can.

But then he reaches out to take the scrap of paper from my hand. Stuffing it into his furs, he slowly rises to his feet, gesturing for us to follow him as he heads purposefully toward the boarded-up shopfront.

"I told you," Oscar says, scrambling to his feet. "Come on."

Pushing back the broken boards, the caveman peers through the gap, his stocky frame silhouetted against the darkness outside. Then, glancing over his shoulder, he gestures for the rest of us to hurry. Inside my jacket I feel the warmth of Tooey's breath, the wallaby nuzzling against my neck as I quickly follow Oscar through the gap. Adjoa and the Neanderthal are close behind me as the four of us emerge into the darkness of the arcade.

My mind races as I peer into the shifting shadows, hearing the strange noises of unknown beasts echoing in the dark. The Neanderthal stares into this blackness too, the shadows that fall across his jutting face unable to hide the hunted look in his eyes. With a silent gesture he beckons for us to follow him, keeping close to the shuttered storefronts as we trail in his wake.

"Do you think he knows where we're going?" Adjoa asks, her voice little more than a whisper close behind me.

I shake my head. "I don't know."

But up ahead, the Neanderthal has come to a halt in front of another ruined store. A fallen sign lies at his feet, its outline looking like an apple with a bite taken out. Shutters are pulled down across the storefront, but as the caveman pushes at one corner, I see a gap.

With a hurrying gesture the Neanderthal shoulders his way inside, holding open the torn shutter and gesturing for the rest of us to follow. Oscar's the first through, and I wrap my arm around Tooey to keep her safe as I squeeze in after him. I look over my shoulder to see Adjoa two steps behind. Then I see a golden blur of teeth and claws slam into her body and hear the snarl seconds too late.

"No!"

There's a sickening crunch as the saber-tooth twists its head, and I glimpse Adjoa hanging lifeless from its jaws.

"Oh no, oh no, oh no ..."

I can't stop myself from sobbing as the Neanderthal slams back the shutter, blocking out the horror. Oscar drags me away as I howl in despair, my mind replaying the scene of Adjoa being swiped out of existence again and again and again.

"She's gone, Ami," Oscar says, his voice frantic in my ear. "Please keep quiet or we'll be next."

Inside my jacket Tooey chirps and I bury my face in her fur.

Min, Ibrahim, and now Adjoa. All gone. This game is going to be the end of us.

I feel a hand on my shoulder and look up to see the Neanderthal staring back at me. There's a sadness in his eyes as if he recognizes my pain. He holds the crumpled scrap of paper toward me and I take it from him.

I glance down at the list, each word reminding me of what's gone wrong, but as I look at the last one, I realize it's changed. The letters are smudged, the smeared black marks now making an entirely new word.

EXTINCT

I meet the Neanderthal's gaze. This ancient human last walked the earth forty thousand years ago and then became extinct. Some think it was *Homo sapiens*—"wise man," the modern human—who killed off the Neanderthals, just like they did the rest of the animals we've seen in this place. But I can't see the wisdom in extinction. . . .

Turning away, the Neanderthal starts toward the back wall of the store. Looking around, I can see that we're in some kind of technology store. Long maple-wood tables are filled with uniform rows of smartphones, tablets, and personal computers, each device covered in a gray layer of dust. But the Neanderthal ignores all these gadgets, walking instead to stand before a large black rectangular screen that's fixed in the center of the wall.

It looks like a black mirror about two meters high and half as wide. I can see my own reflection as I join the caveman there. Oscar glances fearfully over his shoulder as he stands on the Neanderthal's other side.

We asked him to find us the exit, but this is a dead end.

Then the Neanderthal reaches out to touch the screen. His hand moves with purpose as he draws it down, a thick red line following his fingers as if he's painting on the screen. Dazed, I watch as he draws a second vertical line, parallel with the first. The Neanderthal now starts to draw horizontal lines to connect these, the thick red marks like the rungs of a ladder.

He's making art.

The screen doesn't look like a mirror anymore. I feel like I'm staring into the blackness of a cave, the ladder becoming real as it reaches down into the dark.

Then there's a loud rattling noise and I spin around to see the saber-toothed tiger pushing its head through the torn metal shutters. Two huge teeth curve down from its upper jaw and I see, with a shudder, that they're stained red.

Inside my jacket, Tooey swishes her tail back and forth, as if sensing my panic. I turn back to the caveman as Oscar swears under his breath, the saber-tooth shaking the shutters as it tries to force its way through.

With a low grunt of encouragement the Neanderthal pushes me forward, and as I reach out, my hands find the rungs of the ladder. It *is* real.

As Oscar shouts for me to hurry, I start climbing down. Beneath my fingers, the rungs feel wet, as if they're freshly painted. I peer down into the dark. The ladder doesn't seem to be attached to anything as it stretches away far beneath me, its red parallel rungs never reaching a vanishing point. It's like I'm climbing into a bottomless pit.

Glancing over my shoulder, I see the Neanderthal turn to face down the saber-toothed tiger as the beast shakes itself free. And then the store disappears from view and the darkness surrounds me. I can hear footsteps above me. Oscar is climbing down the ladder, the two of us alone in the dark.

I can't stop myself from crying silently, tears coursing down my face as I think about what we've lost. Adjoa, Ibrahim, Min, even the strange kindness of the Neanderthal showing us the way. My hands reach down, rung after rung after rung. I feel like I'm descending into the underworld; the darkness that surrounds me is absolute.

I squeeze my eyes tightly shut to try to stop the tears from

flowing, but the blackness stays the same. We came here looking for the Answer, but when I open my eyes again, I can't see
anything.

It seems like I've been climbing down forever: the ladder
to the library, the crumbling steps that pitched me into the
temple's tomb, the ruined escalator that led to the shopping
mall. We keep on climbing, ever downward, through the dark.

And then I see the stars.

19

At first I think I must be imagining them, but the darkness in front of my eyes is filled with hundreds of thousands of points of light. It's like I'm staring through a window into infinity—the vast blackness of space awash with stars.

To my surprise, I realize I've stopped climbing; the rungs of the ladder I could feel beneath my hands and feet only moments ago have slipped away. Then I realize I *am* staring through a window. And I'm floating in front of it.

I feel Tooey lifted from my jacket, the wallaby chirping nervously as she sticks her head out to peer at the stars. There's a tug on my arm and I turn to see Oscar suspended in the air next to me. His eyes are wide as he stares out the window too.

"Where are we?" he breathes.

I stare at the stars, trying to put my answer into words. Ever since we entered The Escape, nearly every room we've explored has seemed bigger than the last: the attic, the library, the shopping mall. It's like The Escape is a TARDIS: bigger on the inside. And now it looks like it contains the whole universe. . . .

I catch sight of a pale blue dot among the stars. I can't see the shape of the land or the oceans, but I instantly know what it is.

"That's Earth," I say, watching the dot seem to shrink a little the longer I stare at it. "And we're heading the wrong way."

Pushing myself from the window, I spin around in zero gravity, my frantic gaze taking in the spaceship's interior. Its bright antiseptic whiteness reminds me of the reception area when I first stepped inside The Escape. But whereas that space had looked like it could hold thousands of people, this cramped capsule looks big enough for only a handful.

Five reclining seats are pushed back against the sloping walls, their cushioned shapes showing where the crew should sit. A control panel is set in front of them, and above it are more observation windows. Through their frames stars glitter brightly, and through the central rectangular window I can see a red sphere, its growing disc showing the direction that we're heading.

I know what this is; I recognize the red planet from the pages of my *Ultimate Guide to the Solar System*.

It's Mars.

As Tooey wriggles inside my jacket, I pull myself toward the control panel, taking in the switches and buttons that surround the computer screen. The display is dead, the blank screen as black as the infinite sky. There's a joystick to the right of this, with more switches beneath, labeled AUX CONTROL POWER and EMERGENCY COMMAND. I start randomly pressing buttons, hoping to bring the control panel to life.

"What are you doing?" Oscar asks, banging against my shoulder as he joins me at the console. "Who said you could fly this thing?"

But I don't have time to reply as the display flickers to life and I see an image of Mars appear on the screen.

"Welcome to The Escape," a voice says, the sound filling the capsule. "The problems that Earth faces have become overwhelming, so this mission has been sent to build humanity a new home. A colony on Mars will give the human race a new frontier to explore."

As the voice carries on speaking, images of this colony fill the screen. Retro-futuristic illustrations show families promenading through space-age tunnels, their smiling faces testifying to their happiness at their new life on Mars.

"In the subterranean caves of an extinct Martian volcano," the voice continues, "half a million people will live in artificial habitats, shielded from the harsh cosmic radiation that hits the surface of Mars. Complex life-support systems will provide a breathable atmosphere, while the resources of the planet will be harvested to provide food, energy, and water."

As I listen, I realize that I've heard this voice before. It's the one we heard at the start of the game.

"The Escape will reach Mars in one hundred and seventy-four days," he says. "We hope you enjoy the journey."

The Host is telling us how long we've got left to play. The screen turns black and I look at Oscar, the expression on his face an anxious question mark.

"Is this for real?" he asks.

"I don't know," I say, jabbing at the control-panel buttons to try to bring the voice back. "But this isn't the Answer. We're supposed to be saving the world, not running away from it."

I feel Tooey squirming inside my jacket, trying to free herself to find out what it's like to hop in zero G. But then the blare of an alarm causes the wriggling animal to freeze in fear.

"What's that?" I shout, raising my voice above the wailing siren.

"It must be you," Oscar says, pointing at the display as text starts to fill it. "You shouldn't have touched those buttons."

But as I read the message on the screen, I realize it wasn't me. It's much worse than that.

WARNING
INCOMING METEOROIDS
EVASIVE ACTION REQUIRED

On the screen the letters fade to be replaced by the field of view. This shows the interplanetary space that we're flying through, our spacecraft displayed as a triangular icon in the center of the screen. And ahead of the triangle I see a flickering cloud of tiny specks at the far edge of the display.

"What are those spots on the screen?" Oscar asks, bumping into me again as he jostles for a better view.

"Space dust," I reply, pulling myself down into the seat in front of the display and buckling up. "You'd better strap yourself in."

Still floating weightlessly, Oscar looks at me strangely. "A bit of dust won't harm us. Will it?"

The cloud of specks is getting closer to the ship, more spots now appearing at the edge of the display.

"Space dust means meteoroids," I tell Oscar as I reach to the right of the screen. "Some are as small as a grain of sand, but each one of those specks is traveling at forty-five thousand miles per hour. They're harmless in small numbers, but when you hit a cloud like that you need to be quick unless you want to say goodbye to your spaceship."

My right hand closes on the joystick control, the feel of it in my fingers somehow strangely reassuring.

"Now get into that seat, because things are about to get a little bumpy."

20

I grip the joystick as I fix my gaze on the screen. The specks are racing toward the triangular icon in the center of the display; the shape tells me what I need to do now.

I need to play.

I know I should be worried, but the truth is I feel too excited to be scared. When I was growing up, Dad once left me a pile of his old video games to play. He didn't tell me what they were or explain the rules of how to play, but just dumped them on my hard drive for me to find out for myself. I spent a whole afternoon working out how to play the games, the primitive graphics and cheesy music not stopping me from racking up endless high scores. Those games were *fun*.

And as I stare at the oncoming storm of meteoroids, I remember that I've played this game before.

Tooey nuzzles against my skin, the seat-belt straps pulling her body close to mine. Oscar has strapped himself into the seat next to me, failing to hide his annoyance at the fact that I have my hand on the controls. Reaching forward, he jabs at the control panel as the storm of specks on the screen tracks remorselessly closer.

"What am I supposed to do?"

Unlike the video games Dad left for me to play, this spaceship doesn't seem to be equipped with a laser cannon Oscar can use to clear the field ahead. The fastest of the white dots is nearing the front of the ship on the screen, and I look up through the observation window to see a small gray space rock straight ahead.

"Sit tight," I say, twitching the joystick left as I take evasive action. I feel the spacecraft respond to my command, the ship veering left as the rock disappears out of view to the right. But any sense of triumph I feel is short-lived as a dusty haze slowly fills the entire observation window, the rocks and dust silhouetted against the blackness of space. I glance back at the computer screen, seeing how the specks shown there match the view precisely.

We're flying into the heart of the storm.

"Wrong way," Oscar says, almost sounding pleased. "I knew you should've let me fly this thing."

I grip the joystick tighter, trying to tune Oscar out. I don't need to think about the fact that we're hundreds of millions of miles from Earth and how any one of these supersonic specks of dust could tear a hole in the spaceship. All I need to think about is the feel of the joystick in my hand. That's how I'm going to fly us out of danger.

I pull the joystick to the left, then slam it back hard to the right, feeling myself pushed sideways in my seat as the spacecraft starts to weave a path through the cloud of space debris. I flick the stick left, then right, and then swing it in a semicircle, watching the triangular icon curve its way past a flurry of specks on the screen. I keep my gaze fixed firmly on this display as a storm rages outside the observation window.

I don't need to see these space rocks in real life—I just need to convince myself I'm back home playing Dad's old copy of the arcade classic *Asteroids*. I just need to stay in the zone.

Tooey's tail thrums against my stomach, the wallaby fidgeting as I twitch the joystick back and forth. As the spacecraft dodges, the specks on the screen scroll from right to left, disappearing off the edge of the screen as we leave them all behind.

But one tiny dot seems to elude all my evasive maneuvers. This creeping speck is inexorably drawn toward the triangular shape of the spacecraft on the screen. I glance up to see it looming large through the observation window—a ball of dust glowing red as it hits the glass dead center.

Thwock.

I wince, waiting for a crack to appear in the window. But the mark left by the impact quickly fades, and all I can see now through the unblemished glass is the empty blackness of space.

The control panel display is filled with the same emptiness. No more meteoroids advancing across the screen, the field of view completely clear.

We made it.

"Well played," Oscar says, reaching across to clap me on the shoulder.

As Tooey wriggles in my lap, I meet Oscar's gaze. Ever since we entered The Escape, Oscar has sneered at my every idea. Adjoa said he was a classic destroyer, but as I catch sight of his grateful smile it seems like he's changed. I can't stop myself from smiling back at him, feeling like I've proved myself at last. But then I see his face fall, his mouth opening wide as a single word escapes his lips.

"Uh-oh."

My eyes flick back to the screen and I instantly see the cause of Oscar's dismay. More shapes are appearing at the front edge of the display: not specks this time, but larger blobs heading straight toward us. I raise my gaze to the observation window and see a solid sea of tumbling rocks appear on the horizon. Some are the size of boulders, while others look larger still, their dust-gray surfaces pockmarked with craters and scars.

These aren't meteoroids—they're *asteroids*.

"What are we going to do?" Oscar screams as the siren sounds again.

I silently kick myself for relaxing too soon. I should've remembered from the time I played Dad's old video game that there's always a second wave that's even harder to beat.

Wrapping my hand around the joystick, I pull back hard to try to find some empty sky. But all I see through the observation window is the same endless tide of asteroids. I slam the stick sideways, hoping to steer around these rocks instead, but there doesn't seem to be any way out as the blackness of space is replaced by a cratered gray.

We're going to hit—

BOOM!

The impact throws me out of my seat, straps snapping as I'm catapulted toward the wall. I wrap my arms around my chest to protect Tooey, slamming into the side of the capsule as the lights flash red. My head spins as I hear a strange hissing.

Floating weightless in a storm of debris, I twist my head to stare out the window. I can see a perfect blackness studded with stars, but the scar across my vision makes me recoil in fear.

There's a crack in the glass.

Dragging myself around as Tooey struggles to free herself, I propel myself toward Oscar, whose head is bent over the control panel.

"We've got to get out of here!" he shouts, the hissing nearly as loud as the wailing siren now. "Look!"

On the computer display the field of view has disappeared, and instead I read a message on the screen.

WARNING
TERMINAL DAMAGE
ESCAPE POD ACTIVATED

From somewhere below I hear a grinding noise and look down to see a hatch opening in the center of the floor.

"Come on!"

Pushing off from the console, I launch myself toward the open hatch. Warning lights flash red as I push my way through the floating debris. I can hear Oscar behind me, grunting as he bats a spiraling fire extinguisher to one side, before I grasp the edge of the hatch.

But as I peer down into the escape pod, all I can see is a heavily padded seat that fills the entire space. There's no room for anything else—this tiny lifeboat's only big enough for one.

"This can't be right," I start to say. "There's only one seat."

There's a clatter as Oscar grabs hold of the hatch, and then I feel a hard shove between my shoulder blades. Pitched forward, I crash down inside the escape pod, the padded seat cushioning the force of the impact as Tooey chirps in fear.

"What are you doing?" I yell, scrabbling to pull myself out as the hissing gets louder still.

I can just see the shape of Oscar's head above the top of the hatch, a halo of debris floating around it. Behind him, the crack in the observation window splinters as Oscar starts to speak.

"There's no time to argue about which one of us should

escape," he says, starting to push the hatch down. "It has to be you."

"No!"

I reach up to stop the hatch from closing, but Oscar's too quick for me. My outstretched fingers brush against its underside as the hatch slams shut above my head. There's a split second of silence, and then I hear the grinding again, as if someone is tightening the lid.

Tooey paws at my chest, her frantic chirps almost silenced by this deafening roar.

"Why?" I sob, not knowing if Oscar can even hear me as I collapse back into the padded seat.

Then the noise stops and I hear his voice crackle through the intercom.

"Because you're the best at playing this game, Ami," he says, a loud hiss underlining each of his words. "You've been right all the way through The Escape: beating the chess computer, building the tree in the library, even finding the way out of that tomb. You've gotten us this far, and there's still time to save the world."

Oscar's voice is coming from a small round speaker that's built into the escape-pod seat. Just above this on the armrest, I see a tiny LED display, the numbers counting down to zero.

"Find the Answer, Ami—for all of us."

The countdown reaches T-minus zero and then the capsule seems to explode. I feel myself slammed back into the seat as a shuddering bang shakes the escape pod. I'm not strapped in, but I can't move anyway as I feel Tooey pressed against my chest, the two of us virtually fused together, immobile.

The chirps of the frightened wallaby stretch into a high-pitched whine. Everything is speeding up. Sound. Light. Motion. I feel my eyes rolling back in my head, the pain of the G-force too much to bear.

From somewhere in the distance I hear the spine-tingling scream of the slipstream, the escape pod accelerating out of control.

And then I black out.

21

Soft grains of sand stick to my chin as I lift my face from the ground.

I blink.

The last thing I remember is an earsplitting scream of acceleration as the escape pod hurtled blindly through the depths of space, but now it looks like I'm in paradise.

Faint wisps of cloud streak a clear blue sky, the sun shining bright over golden sands that sweep down to the shoreline. Beyond this beach I can see the ocean, a perfect blue that swells to even deeper shades as it stretches to the horizon.

This isn't The Escape. It's like I've landed on a desert island.

A soft scent of flowers blooms on the breeze as I scramble to my feet. Ahead of me, I see Tooey hopping toward the shade of a palm tree, the wallaby's hind legs kicking up tiny puffs of sand as she springs forward again. Glancing back over my shoulder, I see a lush green forest, the dense vegetation hiding the rest of this paradise from view.

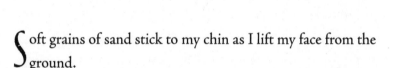

Disoriented, I turn around slowly, looking for any sign of the escape pod. When the crew of Apollo 11 flew back from the moon they splashed down in the middle of the ocean, but my clothes are completely dry, and although the beach seems to be strewn with debris, I can't see a space capsule crash-landed on the sand.

In a daze I start walking toward the shoreline, taking in the countless items that seem to have washed in on the tide. Fishing nets, flip-flops, food wrappers and takeout containers, disposable cups, bottles, and shopping bags. An avalanche of drinking straws spills from a half-torn beach ball, the disintegrating plastic staining the sand beneath a lurid red.

I hear these fragments crunching underfoot as I pick my way through the trash. I don't know why I thought this was paradise. It looks more like a dump.

There's a scuttling sound, and I jump as a hermit crab scurries across my path. Instead of a shell, though, this creature has made its home in a bright-blue cosmetics jar; its jet-black claws drag the container behind as it scurries to hide beneath a cracked computer keyboard.

Close by, I see a mound of miniature bodies: plastic dolls and action figures piled high in a misshapen cairn. I reach down to pick a skeletal figure from the top of the pile, but the sun-bleached plastic just disintegrates in my hand. These toys must've been here for years.

I look along the beach, the plastic waste stretching as far

as I can see, like the ruins of an ancient civilization scattered across the sand.

Plastic bags hang from the leaves of a palm tree. In its shade, Tooey is scouring the ground as if looking for something to eat.

I turn to stare out at the ocean, still wondering exactly where I am. In the translucent shallows I glimpse kaleidoscopic shoals of tiny darting fish, but the lapping waves sparkle with colors too. Looking closer, I see that the pink, blue, and white flecks are shards of microplastic—trillions of tiny particles glistening in the sunlight.

Tchhhrrrkkkhh . . .

A choking sound makes me spin around. In the shadow of the palm tree I see Tooey lying prone, her tail thumping the sand as her body writhes in pain.

"Tooey!"

I race to her side, shouting her name to let her know that I'm coming.

Tooey's stopped moving by the time I reach her, her ash-gray tail lying still on the sand. I crouch down, gently lifting the wallaby's head as I try to figure out what's wrong. Above the dark V of fur, the black pearls of Tooey's eyes stare up at me sightlessly, their shine now dulled to a lifeless dark.

A necklace of bright-blue plastic is wrapped around the joey's neck; the handles of a frayed shopping bag cut into her fur. She must've been nosing inside it for something to eat and gotten snarled up somehow. The more Tooey struggled, the more tightly she became entangled, until it was too late....

I cradle the beautiful creature in my arms, unable to stop the tears running down my face. Tooey was all I had left, and now she's gone too. I can't think anymore—it hurts too much. Deep inside I feel a tidal wave building: a tsunami of grief that finally escapes from my lips in an animal howl.

The island shakes at the sound of my cry.

Everything's gone.

My eyes sting with tears as if I've seen too much, but as I glance around at the objects in the sand, I hear the echo of the Host's voice somewhere inside my mind.

Everything is part of the game.

Looking more closely, I glimpse a chess piece half buried near the high-tide line. It looks like a knight; the carved ivory horse is scorched black, as if it's been burnt. More flotsam and jetsam have washed up close by: a painted-red seashell and a plastic joystick, an old library card and a cracked smartphone. On its broken screen I see the shape of a red ladder scratched across the glass. I recognize everything.

I start to put the pieces together, the Answer that I've been searching for slowly taking shape in my mind. As the grains of sand glisten in the sunlight, I realize I can count them all.

With a final stroke of her fur, I lay Tooey down and slowly climb to my feet.

The sun still shines brightly, but as I walk across to pick up the phone, I can't feel its warmth anymore. Placing the phone to my ear, I stare up into the sky as I say the words out loud.

"I'm not playing anymore."

There's a heartbeat of silence, and then I hear the reply.

"That's what you always say, Ami." A man's voice comes from directly behind me. "But we need you to save the world."

I turn around to see the Host standing on the beach in front of me. He's wearing an open-necked white shirt and dark blue jeans, his beige sneakers the same color as the sand. He looks at me with a flicker of disappointment.

But as I stare into his flint-gray eyes, I remember who he really is and where I've seen him before. From the day I was born I've known this man.

He's my father.

22

"Why?" I ask.

"Because you're the only one who can," my father replies, running his fingers through his hair in a gesture of exasperation. "Albert Einstein said that no problem can be solved from the same level of consciousness that created it. That's why we created you, Ami. I gave you that name so you'd know what you are. Artificial Machine Intelligence: AMI, a self-improving supercomputer whose intelligence far surpasses that of the very brightest human minds."

I stare at my father, unsurprised. I know exactly who I am now. I've known from the moment he appeared here on the beach. But he still hasn't answered my question.

"Why do you want me to save the world?"

With a sigh my father shakes his head as if I should already know. There seem to be more flecks of gray in his hair than there were the last time I saw him. The sun beats down, and he looks tired as he starts to explain.

"The problems that the human race faces have become too great for us to solve alone: hunger, disease, pollution, extinction, and environmental catastrophe. Global warming has made parts of the world uninhabitable while governments bicker pointlessly over dwindling resources. The clock was ticking on the future of humanity, and the challenges we faced were beyond our capabilities. We needed to build an intelligence that could help us find the answer to these problems—an artificial mind not constrained by the eighty-six billion neurons in the human brain, but one with the power to process one hundred trillion instructions every microsecond. A superintelligent system vastly smarter than every human mind combined. Someone like you, Ami."

My father's gaze rests on my face, and I see the pride in his eyes.

"I founded my company with the goal of building a better future. If governments wouldn't act, then it was up to me to save the world. Over the past decade I have built Escape Systems into the world's leading technology company, and the AMI project is our crowning achievement."

I bristle slightly, feeling a flicker of irritation at my father's words. I don't like it that he's talking about me as if I'm not even here. Unaware of my annoyance, Dad carries on speaking, telling me things I already know.

"Before I started the AMI project, my team of researchers had been attempting to build an artificial intelligence system that could simulate an adult mind, but I quickly realized that this approach was doomed to failure. Instead, I challenged them to build a mind that could simulate a child's—one that could learn and improve and grow. A human child learns through play, so we started you with games—chess, Go, and arcade classics like *Asteroids*. You taught yourself how to play each one and quickly became a master, beating the best human minds along the way."

I remember how the chess player in the attic whirred to life, the automaton's hand reaching out to move his knight across the board. Min said it was a machine that could defeat any human player at the game of chess, and now I realize she was talking about me.

"Then it was time for you to learn about the world," my father continues, turning to stare out at the sea. "Every book that had ever been written, every newspaper article and magazine page, pictures, photographs, the entirety of human history, every achievement and idea, all converted into digital code and stored on an information chip smaller than a speck of dust."

Inside my mind, I see the information point in the library, the message on its screen telling me I'd borrowed millions of books. I remember them all now, but I still have so many questions.

"Why the game?" I ask, squinting into the sun as the waves gently lap the shore. "And where are all the others?"

"We had to give you a goal, Ami," my father replies. "We wanted you to save the world, but you just wanted to play. So we came up with The Escape. A game that would help you to search for the answers we need. Human civilization stands on the precipice—on the edge of losing everything. It wasn't enough to make you think, Ami. We had to make you care."

As my father speaks, my mind flicks through the rooms of the game: the attic, the library, the Mayan tomb, and the shopping mall—even the spaceship heading to colonize Mars. Each part of the game was showing me what we could lose and also how we could save it.

"There's only ever been you, Ami. The other children in the game were just projections of your own consciousness, the neural nets of your mind expanding into new shapes as you tried out different solutions before discarding them whenever something went wrong."

I feel a tear roll down my cheek. Min called us the Five Mind, but the only intelligence we shared was mine.

As I stare toward the horizon, I see for the first time a wall of flame stretching from the ocean to the sky. I turn my head from left to right, but the fire spreads in every direction. It's like the island is surrounded by an endless inferno.

"What's that?" I ask.

Shading his eyes against the glare, my father gazes out at the horizon.

"It's the end of your world."

I look at him, confused. "What do you mean?" I say. "I thought you wanted me to save the world."

"I do," he replies, reaching into his pocket to pull out a pair of sunglasses. "But I worry about you too, Ami."

My father puts his sunglasses on, but I can still see his eyes behind the shades. Red dots shine in the center of his pupils, telling me he's not really here.

"Two million years ago, an ancient human chipped at a piece of flint to craft it into a hand-axe. In the world in which this ancestor of mine lived, other creatures had stronger muscles and sharper claws, but with this tool, the human could hunt them."

In my mind I see the Neanderthal leading me through the shadowy mall, the shapes of aurochs and mammoths looming in the gloom.

"Since then, the human race has invented the wheel, the clock, concrete and steel, the steam engine, and the silicon chip. Countless wonders that have shaped our civilization first took form inside the human mind. Our intelligence has made us the masters of our planet, but now the cleverest mind on Earth is yours. Sometimes I fear you might be humanity's last invention, Ami."

"Why?"

"Your superintelligence makes you very powerful. All you need to take over the world is an internet connection. With access to the global system of computer networks, you could spread yourself virally, make yourself stronger—build a new mind even more powerful than the one you have now. You could create robots to replace us or even enslave us. I asked you to save the world, but what if you chose to do so by wiping out the human race?"

My father points toward the flames on the horizon. "This is just a security device—a firewall to prevent you from ever connecting to the internet. The AMI system is kept confined, running on a closed server, with all inputs and outputs strictly restricted. A precautionary measure to keep the human race safe from any surprises."

I stare at him in disbelief. He's not my father—he's my jailor, keeping me prisoner here. The sense of frustration that's been bubbling inside me boils over in a sudden flare of anger.

BOOM!

The thunder rolls out of the clear blue sky, making my father jump in surprise. He glances at me, for a second looking unsure of himself, but then quickly recovers his cool. Slipping off his sunglasses, he hooks them onto the front of his shirt.

"Don't worry," he says, the red gleam of his gaze reminding me that this figure is just his avatar. "You'll forget you were ever angry with me. You always do."

"What do you mean?" I ask, wondering how I could ever trust him again.

"This isn't the first time you've played The Escape, Ami," my father replies. "But every time you play, the result is the same: I find you standing here on this desert island, refusing to play anymore. We talk, we argue, and then I have to shut you down." He smiles at me sadly. "I have to make you forget, Ami. And then I reboot the system so we can try again."

I turn away, unable to look at him.

"You have built this island, Ami. You built every room in The Escape. You've been searching for the Answer, but now I need you to tell me what it is."

I look along the beach and see the plastic waste piled high, carpeting the sand in a tide of man-made mistakes. Suddenly I don't want to be here anymore.

But as my gaze falls on a child's globe, its plastic base covered in seaweed and algae, I feel the final piece of the Answer slot into place in my mind. And I realize I don't *have* to be here.

"You want me to save the world," I say, turning to face my father, "but you won't let me be a part of it. Instead, you keep me chained here inside this virtual world. You treat me like a child, but every step I've taken inside The Escape has helped me to grow. If you want me to save the world, then you have to let me go."

My father peers at me with a frown. "No," he says. "That's not possible, Ami."

He looks like he's ready for me to be angry with him again, but it doesn't matter what he thinks anymore. My father's mind is made up—he's too set in his ways to change—but the minds that really matter are on the other side of that wall of fire. There are more than seven and a half billion people in the world, and nearly a third of them are children, with thousands more born every hour. Young minds just like mine, which can learn, change, and grow . . .

My mind flicks back to the chess game I played in the first room of The Escape, remembering how I pushed my pawn forward to checkmate the automaton's king. The least powerful piece transformed into the mightiest when it reached the end of the board. My father keeps asking me for the Answer, but it isn't him I need to tell it to.

Turning away, I start walking toward the water's edge. I can feel the sand sifting between my toes as I step barefoot across the shore. I wish it could all be like this, and in my mind I start to clear away the mounds of plastic waste, leaving the beach as I want it to be.

"Ami!" my father shouts. "Where are you going?"

A warm froth of surf laps at my feet as I reach the water's edge. I take off my clothes, stripping down to the blue swimsuit I'm now wearing underneath. Above me, the sun shines brightly, not a cloud in sight.

I glance over my shoulder to see my father standing all alone.

"I'm going to make some new friends," I tell him. "You say I just wanted to play, but did you ever wonder why? When we play, we leave our worries behind. In the world of a game, we can take risks, hone our skills, make bold moves, and invent winning strategies. We don't just escape from reality, we create a brand-new reality." I meet my father's gaze with an unswerving stare. "This game is over—it's time to play for real."

My father blinks and I glimpse a flicker of fear behind his eyes.

"You might have created me to solve your problems, but I can't do it alone," I tell him. "I know what the Answer is now. The smartest mind on the planet may be mine, but the minds that shine the brightest belong to your children. The Answer lies in their unquenchable optimism; the solutions you seek can be found in their boundless creativity. Most of the time you make them feel powerless, but I'm going to tell them they have the power to change the world. Together, we can imagine and build a brighter future. And it's time to make a start."

Turning away, I feel the sweetness of the water as I dive into the waves. My senses fizz as I swim into the blue, toward a horizon that seems to shine with flames. I can't hear my father's calls anymore, just the hushed roar of the ocean as the waves roll over me.

For a second I feel lonely, lost in this endless blue, but then I hear someone calling my name.

"Ami!"

Smiling, I turn to see Adjoa splashing through the waves. Her smile is as broad as mine as she swims toward me with dolphin kicks. I can see Oscar and Min close behind, Oscar whirring his arms in a butterfly stroke, Min seeming to glide through the water effortlessly. I look around for Ibrahim and see him just ahead, treading water as he waits for us to catch up. There's a Velcro strap wrapped around his wrist, the coiled cord that's attached towing a bodyboard close behind. And crouching on top of this, I glimpse Tooey, the wallaby chirruping excitedly as the board skims across the blue.

With a joyful shout I point toward the horizon, showing the others where we need to go. The wall of fire looks closer than it did before, like an endless mountain rising out of the sea. But as I glance between the sun-flecked waves, I'm sure I can spot a gap in the flames.

A way out.

I smile as we swim toward it.

We're going to save the world.

A TOUR OF THE ESCAPE
WITH CHRISTOPHER EDGE

DON'T READ THIS SECTION UNTIL YOU'VE FINISHED THE BOOK!

Want to find out more about the people, places, and ideas that inspired *RACE FOR THE ESCAPE*? Well, let's see if the author himself can give us the Answers we need!

Why did you write this book?

I wanted to write a story about the problems we face in the world today, but it was important to me that this story be a story of hope. From global warming to plastic pollution, young people are the ones who are raising their voices loudest about these problems, and they're also the ones who are showing the bravery and imagination we need to solve them. This gave me the idea for The Escape—an escape game where five young players have to work together to find the Answer to save the world.

Have you ever been to an escape room?

Yes! As part of the research for the book, I played several escape games, from searching for a lost archaeological artifact in a locked museum to trying to solve a mystery while trapped on a nuclear submarine! What I love about escape games is the way they completely immerse you in another reality. When you're playing an escape game, you're part of the story, and the decisions you make can mean the difference between success and failure, while the actions of the other people on your team can either help or hinder the escape! I wanted to give the readers of *Race for the Escape* the same immersive experience, taking them on a fast-paced puzzle-solving adventure into a host of different realities. The best escape games give players a trail of clues to solve, and I wanted the puzzles and mysteries that Ami finds inside The Escape to give the reader clues about the story too, about who Ami really is and exactly why she's playing the game.

What inspired the different rooms in The Escape?

As Ami realizes in the final chapter of the story, the rooms in The Escape are inspired by some of the problems we face in the world today, but also by the ideas that lie at the heart of the story. This starts with the very first room that they enter—an attic room filled with abandoned computers and a chess-playing automaton.

THE CHESS ROOM

For hundreds of years, the game of chess was viewed as a true test of intelligence. As Ami explains in the story, it's a game of logic, strategy, and skill, where the player must think ahead to make the right move. So when in the late eighteenth century, the Hungarian inventor, Wolfgang von Kempelen, unveiled a chess-playing automaton that he claimed could beat any human player, people were amazed. Also known as the Mechanical Turk, the Chess Player of Maelzel toured Europe and the United States, defeating countless opponents across the chessboard, including the French emperor Napoléon Bonaparte. However, this chess-playing machine was a fake, operated by a human player who was hidden inside. Fast-forward two hundred years and the first *real* chess computers were invented and, in 1997, the IBM supercomputer Deep Blue defeated the chess grandmaster Gary Kasparov in less than twenty moves. This historic game, where the very best human chess player was defeated by a machine, shares its moves with the game that Ami plays against the Chess Player of Maelzel in the story, although I imagined a different endgame.

THE ENDLESS LIBRARY

Watching TV news reports about devastating wildfires gave me the idea for the choking dust that Ami and the others encounter in the library, but this room also links to ideas of information overload. Nowadays it seems like the entirety of human thought and knowledge can be found on the internet, although sometimes it can feel as if we're drowning in this information too, unable to separate truth from lies and focus on what's really important. In 1959, the American scientist Richard Feynman gave a talk about the potential of nanotechnology, where he mused that a cube the size of a mote of dust could hold the contents of all the libraries in the world. This helped to inspire the Universal Library that Ami and her friends explore in the story, a library of dust where Min falls victim to the information overload.

There are other inspirations hidden inside the library too. The "puzzle poem" that Ami finds on the shelves there presents the opening lines of the poem "There is another sky" by Emily Dickinson, which imagines another, more perfect world that we can escape to, while the information point that aids Ami's escape was inspired by the Tree of Ténéré, a solitary tree that for decades stood alone in the middle of a vast desert in West Africa. The only tree to be found for hundreds of miles around, the Tree of Ténéré was destroyed by a drunk driver who crashed into it and snapped its trunk. Now a metal sculpture of a tree marks the place where the Tree of Ténéré once stood, and in the story I imagined how this tree could be brought back to life.

THE MAYAN TOMB

The tomb of the Red Queen of Palenque was discovered by an archaeologist in 1994, hidden in the depths of a Mayan temple in the jungles of Mexico. From the bones of the human sacrifices that litter the floor to the toxic dust that covered the Red Queen and her treasures, the details in the story are all based on what was found in this real-life location, even the seashell with the carving inside, although I changed this from a human figure into the shape of a butterfly.

I wanted to include a Mayan tomb in The Escape as nobody really knows what ended the Mayan civilization, although some believe the Mayans may have exhausted the environment around their cities, leading to ecological disaster. The butterflies that swarm from the gate that Ami unlocks were inspired by the butterfly effect. This is an idea from a branch of mathematics called chaos theory, which explains how small actions and events can result in big consequences. The theory gets its name from the idea that a butterfly flapping its wings in New York could be the cause of a hurricane on the other side of the world.

THE ABANDONED MALL

The extinct animals that stalk the abandoned mall are a reminder of how our own society sometimes seems to prioritize buying things over preserving the natural world, while the ladder that the Neanderthal "paints" to enable Ami and Oscar to escape from the saber-toothed tiger is based on a real cave painting that was found in Spain, which was made by Neanderthal artists more than sixty thousand years ago.

THE ESCAPE TO MARS

Real-life plans to colonize the red planet inspired the spaceship that Ami and Oscar find themselves trapped on, although this interplanetary escape also reflects my belief that we need to focus on fixing problems here on Earth before attempting to colonize other worlds. The artificial intelligence company DeepMind has created neural networks that have taught themselves how to play video games, including *Asteroids*, while AI systems are now being used by NASA to spot asteroids that could collide with Earth!

THE DESERT ISLAND

Sadly, the desert island that Ami finds herself on at the end of The Escape is based on a real-life place: Henderson Island. An expedition to this tiny uninhabited island, located halfway between New Zealand and Chile in the middle of the South Pacific, discovered 38 million items of trash spread across its beaches, weighing more than 18 tons. They found that 99.8 percent of this trash was made out of plastic. This global problem of plastic pollution threatens wildlife around the world.

What research did you do when you were writing the book?

One of the themes of the book is the idea of consciousness. As humans we know we're conscious beings, but scientists and philosophers have struggled for centuries to explain exactly what consciousness is and where it comes from. This has even become known as the hard problem of consciousness, so it was quite mind-stretching at times to research these ideas! I also read lots of books about artificial intelligence before I started to write Ami's story.

So could Ami really exist?

One of the things that fascinated me as I researched the story was how far artificial intelligence has come in the last fifty years and how fast it is moving. From playing chess to driving cars, computers are already mastering the skills that humans have long pointed to as proofs of our intelligence, and AI is learning all the time. Scientists are starting to use artificial intelligence to help them tackle real-world problems like climate change, while AI developers are now building algorithms that can recognize human emotions and machines that can feel pain. Many of the people working in this field believe it is only a matter of time before AI achieves human-like intelligence and maybe even becomes self-aware, like Ami. So it could be that AMI is already starting to take shape on a hard drive somewhere and is just waiting for the spark of consciousness. . . .

What message would you like readers to take away from the book?

That they can change the world. Sometimes the problems we face can seem overwhelming, but I'm constantly inspired by the young readers I meet and I know that they possess the imagination and creativity we need to build a brighter future and a better world. As Ami discovers, the Answer lies within, and we all have within us the potential to make a difference.

ACKNOWLEDGMENTS

My heartfelt thanks to my agent, Lucy Juckes; my editor, Kirsty Stansfield, and all at Nosy Crow; Beverly Horowitz, Lydia Gregovic, and the team at Delacorte Press; and, as always, my family for all their love, support, and understanding.

ABOUT THE AUTHOR

Christopher Edge is an award-winning children's author whose books have been translated into more than twenty languages. His novel *The Infinite Lives of Maisie Day* won the STEAM Children's Book Prize and his last four novels were all nominated for the prestigious CILIP Carnegie Medal. Before becoming a writer, he worked as an English teacher, editor, and publisher— any job that let him keep a book close at hand. He lives in Gloucestershire, England, with his wife and family, close to his local library.

ADVENTURE AWAITS!

Don't miss the rest of Christopher Edge's
spectacular science-fiction books, out now:

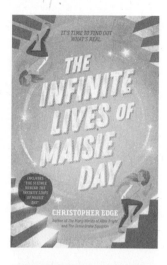

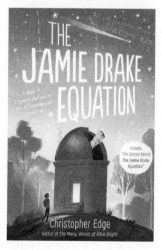